MW01194565

The Truth of the Aleke

"The best fiction leaves us asking difficult questions about the world we live in, and this novella succeeds in doing that and more. Such incredible writing!"

—T. L. Huchu, *USA Today* bestselling author of
The Library of the Dead

"This mind-bending story will have both new and returning fans hooked."

—*Publishers Weekly* (starred review)

"Utomi's searing, thought-provoking fantasy novella has heartbreaking parallels in the present and is highly recommended."

—*Library Journal* (starred review)

"Utomi returns to the Forever Desert with this devastating, timely fantasy novella. . . . There is no solace in this thought-provoking sequel, only uncomfortable truth."

—*Booklist* (starred review)

"*The Truth of the Aleke* feels like you're stepping into a story told around a campfire by a wise elder. We are literally watching an undeniable voice come into his own."

—Maurice Broaddus, author of the Astra Black series

"*The Truth of the Aleke* weaves a dazzling tale that paints with sharp strokes, through massive battles and dizzying magics, to show the sheer power of stories and the deadly confluence between truth and lies."

—Oghenechovwe Donald Ekpeki,
World Fantasy Award–winning editor of *Africa Risen*

THE MEMORY OF THE
OGISI

MOSES OSE UTOMI

TOR PUBLISHING GROUP
NEW YORK

THE MEMORY OF THE OGISI

Copyright © 2025 by Moses Ose Utomi

A Tordotcom Book
Published by Tom Doherty Associates / Tor Publishing Group
120 Broadway
New York, NY 10271

www.torpublishinggroup.com

Tor® is a registered trademark of Macmillan Publishing Group, LLC.

EU Representative: Macmillan Publishers Ireland Ltd, 1st Floor,
The Liffey Trust Centre, 117–126 Sheriff Street Upper, Dublin 1, DO1 YC43

The Library of Congress Cataloging-in-Publication Data
is available upon request.

ISBN 978-1-250-84904-5 (hardcover)
ISBN 978-1-250-84840-6 (ebook)

Our books may be purchased in bulk for specialty retail/wholesale, literacy, corporate/premium, educational, and subscription box use. Please contact MacmillanSpecialMarkets@macmillan.com.

First Edition: 2025

Printed in the United States of America

10   9   8   7   6   5   4   3   2   1

To my parents,
Oseyi Mike Utomi and Stella Odalomhen Uwaibi-Utomi,
who journeyed bravely beyond their City of Lies,
shared generously the water they found,
and prepared me for my own journey
through the Forever Desert.

THE MEMORY OF THE OGISI

EVEN DESERTS HAVE *a beginning.*

Yet no one knows how the city began.

Some say it was born of the earth the way a babe is born of the mother, formed from the ether of creation. Some say it rode down upon a bolt of lightning, embedded whole into the desert sands as the thunder crashed. Some say it was built brick by brick by a little boy with big ears, who was lost for so long that he made a home of his lostness and beckoned others to join him.

Many sought the city's true origins, using the Sight gifted them by the Goddess to peer into the past. Yet the Goddess works mysteriously; rather than Seeing a single story, each of the city's citizens Saw a past unique to them, as different from the others' visions as the swirls on their fingertips.

Hence, the city earned its name: the City of a Thousand Stories.

There soon arose those who sought the truth not by divine vision but by earthly scripture. These great minds scavenged the city for stories of the past, undertaking pilgrimages for partial pages, vast journeys for dusty tomes. In time, these people housed their findings in the Great Temples, the world's greatest repositories of human knowledge.

For their fearlessness, and for their willingness to seek out the city's beginnings, they became known as ogisi: those who seek the truth. Decade by decade, century by century, story by story, the ogisi tirelessly pursued the sacred task of uniting the shattered shards of the city's history, for they understood the dire consequences of their failure: A people who do not learn their past cannot chart their future.

Nevertheless, despite their diligence, the ogisi failed to learn the truth of the city's origins, and it began to appear as if the task was one that would have no end.

But such could not be true.

Even gardens have an end.

In the centuries that passed, a story emerged. Long ago, in the days of the Greatmamas, the city was ruled by the venerable Obasa the Wise. He was a tower of a man, with shoulders broad as a buffalo. Yet he was known not for his strength but his integrity. Leaders from across the Forever Desert told him their secrets, entrusting him with the stories of their people. Eventually, he knew all that could be known and was the wisest man in the world.

Many begged Obasa to share his secrets, but he refused. One day, though, when he was long in his years and nearing life's end, Obasa left the city and went fearlessly into the Forever Desert. He was assailed by the heat, so he drank water to cool himself. He was confronted by monstrous beasts, so he raised his spear and slew them.

Then he came upon a being known simply as the Ajungo. It was the shape of a man but made from sand, as if armored in the desert itself. When it opened its mouth, its voice was the sweetest song ever sung, like warm bread dipped in honey, a song that could calm the most turbulent babe. Yet the Ajungo's voice is the song of oblivion, and Obasa, wise as his name, saw the true horror that awaited him as the song drew to its end. So he cut away his ears rather than let it lure him into its lethal embrace.

Though free of the Ajungo's song, Obasa knew he would not long outlive his injuries. So he took a beautiful black gourd from his belongings and whispered into it all the wisdom he had amassed over the years, including the story of the city's birth. Then he dug a hole deep into the sand and buried all his riches, the black gourd among them.

And with a final satisfied breath, he died.

Five hundred years passed. In that time, many ogisi devoted their lives to finding Obasa's Tomb, lured in equal measure by treasure and truth.

None returned.

It has been nearly a century since any ogisi has ventured beyond the city walls. The citizens of the City of a Thousand Stories eagerly await the day when one of their ogisi will again cast the die of fate, brave the terrifying tongue of the Ajungo, and embark on the quest for Obasa's Tomb.

It is that ogisi whose story we tell. Not the loftiest of ogisi but, rather, the lowliest. Not an ogisi devoted to the study of Obasa, the wisest man who ever lived, but one devoted to the study of Osi, an insignificant man forgotten by history. For it is this ogisi, the most unlikely of all, who embodies the third Memento of the Ogisi.

Even water has a story.

And this is the story of Ogisi Ethike.

PART I
ETHIKE

1

WHENEVER HE WAS IN the Great Temple of Osi, Ethike felt peace.

Unlike the other Great Temples, with their sky-piercing black spires visible from anywhere in the city, the Great Temple of Osi was a cramped closet attached to an abandoned theater. It smelled aged and earthen, its shelves three years past their last dusting. Though all Great Temples were open to the public, the city's people preferred the ease and vividness of Sight to the slow labor of reading written works. Thus, few of the Great Temples saw much use—the Great Temple of Osi least of all.

So, as he did most days, Ethike sat alone at a small desk in his humble temple, lost in a slim text that mentioned Osi. Ethike's obsession with Osi had made him an outcast among the ogisi, a fact he understood and accepted. There was fame and fortune in studying the histories of the city's most important figures: the failed rebel leader Lunha; Illami the Prophet, the first Seer; and, most of all, Obasa the Wise.

But it wasn't fortune and fame that Ethike sought. He was drawn to studying history for philosophical reasons, to test his deeply held conviction that every human was important, from the humblest beggar to the mightiest oba. In Osi, Ethike found the perfect test case. Just because Osi played a scant role in the histories that survived did not mean he played a small role in history.

This particular book was one he'd read dozens of times, fascinated not just by its reference to Osi by name, which was rare enough, but by its use of a moniker that appeared in no other texts—"the last Truthseeker." Ethike had thought about it for years but had never been able to draw any useful conclusions from it.

Until this day.

In the manner of all great insights, it came by its own volition. One moment, Ethike was rereading an old tome with an unclear meaning, and the next, he finally understood, beyond any doubt, what the histories had long been trying to tell him.

He finally had something he could take to the Elders.

Ethike's view of the book was suddenly blocked by the round, hopeful face of a young girl. His niece, Uwi, leaning over the pages. Her smile was the same as always: all teeth, eyelids in a joyful arc, cheeks tight with amusement.

"Uncle Ogisi Ethike," Uwi's fingers signed, "it is late."

Ethike leaned away, exhaling himself out of his theories and back into the real world.

"I am sorry, little camel," he signed back, smiling. The wall clock said ten past the hour. He had gone very late. "Were you waiting long?"

"Yes," she signed, then wagged her hand beside her mouth in laughter. "You do not mind time when you read."

Ethike apologized again, then hurriedly stuffed the book and his papers into his bag.

"Why are you smiling so big, Uncle Ogisi?" Uwi signed. "Did the book make you happy?"

"Yes," he signed back, "very."

With a buoyancy in every step, he led Uwi out of the Great Temple. Just outside, they came across a tattered and refuse-stained beggar sitting on the ground beside a tavern. One of his arms was missing, a sleeve dangling empty at his side.

"Please, honored ogisi, coins for a meal?"

Ethike didn't have any extra coins to give. His decision to devote his life to the study of Osi meant he barely had money to take care of himself and Uwi.

But he wanted to help as best he could. And he wanted to be a good example to Uwi. He reached into his pocket and took out the coin he'd been intending for tomorrow's bread.

"Uncle Ogisi . . ." Uwi signed, placing a hand on his shoulder to stop him.

"What is it?" he replied.

Uwi pointed at the man's hip, just beside his empty sleeve. A small ridge pressed against his khaftan from the inside, like a fist poorly concealed.

"His knuckles," Uwi signed.

Ethike's eyes agreed with Uwi—it did appear that the man's fist was balled beneath his top. But Ethike was a man ruled by his heart, not his eyes. And his heart told him that liars were as deserving of a good meal as honest men.

So Ethike crouched down in front of the beggar and handed over his coin. "May the Goddess guide you," he prayed as Uwi, who loved her uncle, looked on with pity, "and protect you, and forgive you. And may the story of your life be remembered truly."

Then Ethike continued on home, and the beggar took the coin into the tavern, and Ethike never wondered how it was spent.

* . * . *

The trek home took Ethike and Uwi across the city. Past its black brick buildings and beneath the patient green clouds of the city's soaring trees. Through historic parks and over two of the city's three rivers. Overhead, the stars were a spray of white paint on a dark canvas.

The walk home was the part of Ethike's day he loved most. He had experienced a lot of pain in the City of a Thousand Stories—heartbreaks, failures, loneliness, and loss. But when he walked through it, he could only recall the joy. All the opportunities he'd been given, the kindness he'd been shown, the lessons he'd learned, the people who'd brought peace to his heart. He loved the city, and there was nothing better in life than sharing the things you love with the people you love.

For Ethike, that was Uwi. So they took a different route home every day, allowing him to share the city with her, show her new things, or tell her new stories about old things. Watching her hopeful eyes drink in the city's beauty—her small, perfect hand in his, her occasional burp of delighted laughter—was the greatest gift he could ever receive. Each time, it felt like a little part of her unfurled for him to see, and by the time they got home he always felt like he had done something more important than any history he would ever unveil.

Their home was a modest one, all black brick like the rest of the city. Inside, a low ceiling covered just two rooms—one with a bed, the other with a sink. A table near the door held several books Ethike had dragged home from the Great Temple and the latest copy of *The Speaker*, the city's monthly newsletter. Ethike couldn't bring himself to read it—it was mostly gossip—but it was the only writing the people of the city seemed to enjoy, so he felt it important to have around.

They ate a dinner of bread, stew, and beans, then washed up and lay down to sleep, Uwi on her bed and Ethike on his sleep mat.

"Sleep well, little camel," he signed. He leaned over to extinguish their oil lamp, but she halted him with an upraised hand.

"Uncle Ogisi Ethike," Uwi signed, "why did the book make you so happy?"

Ethike smiled. "Because . . ." He tried to think of how to explain it. "It taught me something very important."

"What?"

"The truth," he signed, "I hope."

That made her think for a while. "What will you do with it?" she asked.

"The only thing to do with the truth is to share it."

"With who?"

"With everyone. But the Elders first."

There was another long stretch of her just thinking. Then: "I love you, Uncle Ogisi," she signed, and rolled over into sleep.

Ethike lowered the wick and blew out the lamp, but he stayed awake for a while. For the first time in his career, he had research to present to the Elders themselves. But he also had a lovely life caring for Uwi and being cared for by her. As he reflected on how much there was in his life to be thankful for, it all became too overwhelming.

He cried. Crying had always been, for him, a form of prayer. As a child, he had been ashamed of his tears, of how thoroughly life could dissolve him. But he'd come to learn that crying was the ultimate expression of gratitude: There is no mourning except for that which was beautiful. Perhaps, he thought, the reason it was so hard to sign and cry at the same time was because tears were meant to express what words could not.

Ethike prayed until sleep took him.

2

THE CAPITOL ROSE UP from the elevated plateau near the city's center. It was soft, dark wood, shaped to resemble a tree with its sturdy, square center and mushrooming top. Warm wind whistled between its support pillars, blowing against Ethike as he made his way to the top of the central staircase, where royal guards searched him for weapons before leading him into the throne room.

The marble ceiling was black. The marble floor white. Ahead of him the thirteen Elders sat on identical wooden thrones, clad in rainbow-slashed igbulu, one shoulder bare. Each one of their heads was encased in bronze, a reptilian face etched into the surface. Behind them, a wide slit in the ceiling poured forth a waterfall that streamed endlessly into another opening in the floor.

Ethike prostrated himself, crossing his arms over his chest and touching his head to the floor before he rose to his knees.

"Honored Elders," he signed. "I come to you in humility, beseeching your wisdom."

There was a moment of delay, then all their hands flashed in complete unison. "Our wisdom is yours, Ogisi."

"Honored Elders, I believe I can find Obasa's Tomb."

Stillness. Their faces behind bronze, the Elders betrayed no emotion. But Ethike could feel their skepticism. They knew well the most successful of the ogisi: Ogisi Izio the Clever; Ogisi Hie-hie of the Mighty Mind; the Legendary Ogisi Dallo. They did not know Ethike because he wasn't worth knowing. How could this unknown ogisi from the lowliest temple purport to have an answer that had eluded all the greatest ogisi of the last century?

Even deserts have a beginning, the first Memento of the Ogisi said. Ethike thought that perhaps this would be his beginning.

"Explain," the Elders eventually commanded.

One thing about Obasa's histories had always confused Ethike: Why would Obasa leave his own city to wander the desert? No guards or servants. No emissary sent on his behalf. Many of the histories claimed he was seeking truth, but that made little sense. What truth could there be that the wisest man in the world didn't know?

Then Ethike had found a mention of Osi that called him "the last Truthseeker," and it seemed the answer to all those questions. It was not Obasa the Wise who traveled the Forever Desert, seeking truth and wisdom. It was one of his emissaries. Someone who would rightfully travel alone, with neither guards nor servants. Someone of such low rank that their deeds would be forgotten rather than remembered, retold, chronicled. Someone whose accomplishments, if any, would inevitably be laid at Obasa's feet by history's generous hands.

Ethike told all of this to the Elders, and they watched indifferently, rooted in their thrones. He understood that his proclamation would change his life—for better or worse, he could not know. Because in the City of a Thousand Stories, where each person had a version of history that only they could see, only Obasa the Wise was sacred. Sacred things aren't kind to challengers.

Once Ethike completed his proclamation, the world as he knew it would end.

Even gardens have an end. The second Memento of the Ogisi.

"I believe it is not Obasa's Tomb we must seek," he concluded. "It is Osi's."

Ethike held his breath. Sweat bloomed across his skin.

The Elders watched him with a patient and piercing intent, a row of old owls. Somehow, though they never signed a word to each other, he knew they were conferring.

Then they signed.

"Long has it been since any ogisi was brave enough to seek out Obasa's Tomb. If this ogisi will seek it out, you will be a hero to the citizens, and to your peers. Go, Ogisi, and return with the wisdom of the Forever Desert."

They then all clapped at once, and the vibration sat in the air like a haze of dust.

Before Ethike knew what was happening, he was given a wagon full of supplies—food and clothes, replacement wheels and drums of water. He was given a personal guard—Aza, who was said to be the city's finest soldier. Lastly, he was given a guide—Zogo, the city's wealthiest merchant, who was said to have survived a hundred journeys across the desert.

"Thank you, Elders," Ethike signed. "But . . ." He couldn't believe he was asking for anything more after being given a hero's treatment. But he could not go off saving the city's history while he still had a child to take care of. "My niece. She is just a little girl, and I am the only one to care for her. If I am not here . . ."

The Elders nodded, all together, before replying. "As long as you are away, the child will live here, at the Capitol, and she will be given a life befitting a hero's niece."

Ethike felt tears of gratitude clouding his eyes. How silly he'd been to fear the Elders. He regretted many things in life, but he had never regretted placing faith in other people. And this time was no different.

When he returned home that night and told Uwi of his impending departure, she neither cried nor celebrated. She hugged him and laid her head against his hip for a long while. Ethike was taller than most, but she was already up to his belly, and he had to nearly fold in half to wrap his arms around her and kiss her atop her head.

"My Uncle Ogisi is a hero," she said.

The Elders had demanded that he leave the next morning. At dawn Ethike reported to the city walls, where he was greeted by his new retinue. In the streets below, every citizen of the City of a Thousand Stories had gathered to see him off. He looked out across the city's ebon architecture and emerald forestry, its three gallant rivers and hill-laden topography. Young and old, rich and poor, the people of the city wore their finest clothes, waved the city's black flag, stomped their feet, pounded drums, celebrated the thing they all loved most: a story.

Even water has a story. The third Memento of the Ogisi.

A few times, Ethike thought he found Uwi among the masses, only to realize it was someone else. But no matter. She could see him. She knew what her Uncle Ogisi was doing, and she knew he was doing it for her. Ethike made a twofold promise then: to find Osi's Tomb, and to return to give Uwi the life she deserved.

He wouldn't let her down. He wouldn't let any of them down.

3

EVEN DESERTS HAVE *a beginning.*

Yet Ethike could imagine neither beginning nor end to the Forever Desert. Once the city disappeared past the horizon that first day, Ethike found himself adrift in rolling mounds of gold. For all his life, he'd understood space using the landmarks of the city—a league was the distance from his home to the Great Temple of Asil; his neighborhood was anywhere that carried the aroma of Ihenwele bakery's fresh bread. In the Forever Desert, the only space was the desert itself, a single endless room shared by every living thing.

It was wondrous. Humbling. The city was big, but it was a largeness made and filled by humans. The desert's largeness was just as the histories had portrayed it—mysterious, divine.

"Never has a thing been named so right," Zogo the merchant signed, his fleshy body bouncing in the wagon's driver's seat. He was sharp-eyed and sharp-minded, and from the way he seemed both at ease with and apprehensive toward the desert, Ethike could tell he was as experienced as he was rumored to be. Unlike Ethike, who had to relocate to the wagon's cabin every few minutes to relieve the unbearable itch of his backside, Zogo had been driving for hours with no signs of discomfort. "How long is our journey in these sands, Bookboy?"

"A few weeks, at least," Ethike replied.

Zogo raised an eyebrow. "Ya sound like ya don't know."

Ethike smiled. "The histories are not so precise, unfortunately. As long as the journey is a pleasure, why worry about the length?"

Zogo scowled and made a profane gesture. "The words of a man who has never slept in a proper bed."

Most mentions of Obasa's travels described him venturing south and east by the brightest star. They were less unified on the length of his journey. Some claimed he'd survived in the desert for years; others claimed he'd only lasted a few days. Deducing from the most reliable and consistent sources, Ethike judged that the journey would take just over a month if they kept a steady pace.

Sundown came quickly, and with it came the plunging chill of a desert night. Another desert oddity—in the city, the nights were scarcely any cooler than the days. Zogo called for a short break, during which the soldier, Aza, lit a fire beside the wagon. They sat around it, enjoying some of their rations as Zogo opened the conversation with a great belch of smoke from his chillum pipe.

"So what have ya discovered," the merchant signed with his free hand, "that made the Elders sentence me to such poor company?"

"Well . . ." Ethike replied, scratching his head. He always struggled to explain his research succinctly to non-ogisi. "As you may know, I study at the Great Temple of Osi."

"Who is that?" Zogo asked. "I know my stories and I never heard of this 'Osi.'"

Ethike nodded. "Most people have not. But some pieces of his story overlap with what we know of Obasa. I believe it was Osi who left behind a treasure in the Forever Desert. It is Osi's Tomb we seek."

He'd hoped for some sign of surprise. Instead, Zogo watched Ethike the way a fish watches a drowning man.

Then his skin flared with sparkling light. It was the power of Sight, the Goddess's gift to humanity. Zogo was using it to peer into the past and verify Ethike's claim for himself.

When his skin dimmed, the merchant's eyebrows danced with doubt. "So ya say," he signed. He tipped out his pipe ash into the sand.

Aza's skin flared and diminished as well, and though the stoic guard made no comment, she looked away as if trying to avoid witnessing Ethike's embarrassment.

It was an ogisi's role to seek out and understand the truth. But Ethike knew that most people viewed the ogisi as arrogant know-it-alls, preachers in search of pulpits. Seeing was a direct connection to the Goddess. Pure. Unmediated. It didn't just tell them the truth, it *showed* them the truth. Why trust the fallible words of the ogisi over the divine visions of their own minds?

It came as no surprise, then, that Zogo and Aza doubted him. But he would need their trust if he intended to lead this journey.

Trust is the only coin that doubles when spent, said Osi in one of his few existing quotes. *Spend generously.*

"We should continue," Zogo signed, and Aza leapt to her feet to begin readying the wagon. "While the sun is down."

It wouldn't be easy, Ethike knew, to teach them to trust. But their journey would depend on it. And perhaps their lives.

*   *   *

One day, as a child, Ethike had grown curious about fire. He'd wondered whether fire itself had a smell or whether it simply bore the smell of the things it consumed. So, when his parents lit a fire behind their home to burn some waste, he brought his face as close as he could for a sniff. The flames burned away his eyelashes and scorched his cheeks glassy. That day, he thought he had come to fully understand the danger of heat.

In just a day of travel, the Forever Desert taught him otherwise.

It was not just the sun—or the sand, which seemed to drink greedily of the sun's rays. It was the air itself, no different from that day he'd pressed his face against fire. No matter how much water he drank, he remained dry. No matter how much shade he found, his skin burned.

Zogo looked over at him and smirked around his pipe. "No sun like this in ya dusty temples, eh Bookboy?" he signed.

"Not like this," Ethike admitted with a weak smile, a wet cloth draped over his head.

Zogo motioned understanding but said nothing more.

Ethike spent most of the trip in the wagon's cabin, a clay-lined wooden room designed to keep its inhabitants cool and large enough for four to sit in without touching knees. Aza was lying down across from him in apparent sleep, but would occasionally open her eyes and sign a question:

"Which direction are we traveling?"

"You were born in the east, by Ihenwele bakery?"

"What happens to a Great Temple that has no ogisi?"

At first, Ethike thought the questions were somehow related to their security, but he came to realize that Aza was just curious. She didn't seem to mind his long-winded answers. She would watch him carefully, nodding every so often to show she understood, then lay back her head, close her eyes, and sign "thank you" when the conversation was over.

On the third night, the wagon came suddenly to a stop. Aza was immediately alert. She hopped off the back of the wagon, striding smoothly but rapidly toward the front. Ethike wanted to see what was going on, but he knew his role. Whatever the issue was, if he was needed, they would call for him.

After nearly a minute, Zogo's face popped into view at the back of the wagon.

"Bookboy . . ." he signed. "Ya gon' wanna see this."

4

IT WAS A SMALL TOWN, just a single half-paved road with a few squat buildings on either side. In the dark, it was only visible by the points of light glowing within the buildings. The lights flickered, as if something was passing in front of them.

People.

Ethike had read countless stories of people in the Forever Desert. Books have a way of making fake things seem real, but sometimes they can also make real things seem fake, by elevating only the most sensational of facts. He realized that all he knew of the people of the Forever Desert were such sensationalism. They had become mythical beings in his eyes, strange nomads who braved the monsters and magic of their desert home. Now he could see, with no small bit of shame, that they had always been just as real as he was. While he'd been safe behind the walls of his city, his belly full of water, they'd been out in this furnace of a land, living and loving and suffering for centuries.

Now he was going to meet them. The people from the stories.

"Do you know this place?" Ethike asked.

Zogo shrugged his heavy shoulders. "This desert has many such places. Though I can't say I know of one in this area. The Forever Desert destroys and creates new towns like a fickle god."

"Is it safe?" Ethike pressed.

He shrugged again. "My job is comfortable," he signed before gesturing to Aza. "Safe is her job."

Ethike looked to Aza. "Safe?" he signed again.

"No," Aza signed back. "All those we meet beyond the walls are a risk. I can scout ahead, but I am alone. If I die, you will be unprotected."

"If ya die," Zogo countered, "then ya did ya job. I want a bed and a bath and out of this godsblind heat."

They were divided. The decision was up to Ethike.

As much as he feared making the wrong choice, he was more

excited at the prospect of the right one. The Forever Desert was of course full of monsters, the Ajungo being the worst of them. But these were not monsters; they were people, just like the people of the city. If he could show Zogo and Aza that they could trust these strangers, it would do much to prove his own trustworthiness.

"Aza, scout ahead please," he signed. "We will follow."

* * *

Ethike waited beside Zogo in a dark and narrow alley. Up close, the buildings were compact, ramshackle things made from unstable sand bricks. Chatter leaked out from one building in particular, one slightly wider and more illuminated than the others.

Aza stood outside it, back against the wall, her skin shining with the power of Sight from beneath her black silks. The most common use of Sight was to look into the past. However, it was said that masters of the Seeing Arts—those soldiers, like Aza, who devoted their lives to Seeing—could use it to better perceive the present as well, to enhance their eyes and ears and noses to superhuman levels.

When her skin dimmed, she flashed her fingers across the road to Ethike and Zogo. "It is safe."

Ethike smiled. Of course it was.

He crossed over to Aza, giving the woman a thankful nod, then entered the building.

Inside were long tables and lamplight. Dust floated in the diffuse glow between the patrons, whose fingers fluttered in conversation. It was a simple traveler's lodge. A small and meager one, but in line with what Zogo had suspected. Ethike swept his gaze around the room, unable to keep the wonder from his face. This was a historic moment: He was the first ogisi in a century to lay eyes on people beyond the city walls.

They were beautiful. Tall and short, round and thin, dark-skinned and pale brown. It was a medley of humanity, each person adding to its bounty.

"We're safe," he said, partly to himself and partly to his companions.

But Aza was staring past him, her face morphing further into discomfort by the second.

"What is it?" Ethike asked.

Zogo's chuckle was gurgled gravel. "Soldier girl never been outside her city, eh? It is the ears, Bookboy."

Ethike had to study the room for a while before he understood.

In the City of a Thousand Stories, every infant was entered into the Silence. It was a ritual passed down from Obasa the Wise himself, wherein the ears were cut away and the wound was cauterized to protect them against the deathly song of the Ajungo.

Yet everyone in the lodge had ears. Uncut and unburned, thin flaps sticking out at lengths as varied as the heads that held them. It was an uncomfortable sight, as bizarre as opening the sticky, misshapen mouth of an old man and finding an infant's teeth inside. Ethike had no idea what it meant, but his staring was beginning to earn him stares in return, so he strode toward the nearest table with his most charming smile.

"Hello, friends of the Forever Desert," he signed.

The woman and two men at the table paused their conversation and evaluated him thoroughly. He did his best to keep his eyes off their ears.

"A northerner," the woman signed. She seemed friendly, her hair up in a short tower of braids that spilled outward and her face bearing an open and enthused curiosity. She had the look of someone who was energized by rumors.

Ethike maintained his smile but was taken aback. "Pardon?"

She motioned to his ears. "I have seen your countrymen before. The City of Silence, we call it."

He supposed it was accurate.

"And you all are from?" he asked.

"The east," she signed.

"What is your city called?"

The woman didn't respond. Instead, she shared a look with her companions before peering at Ethike with a half smile. "You are a Tombseeker, are you?"

Ethike's eyes lit up. He had never heard the term, but he liked it. The first person he met in the Forever Desert was just like him.

She smiled at the elation on his face. "As am I," she signed.

She told the story of her city, a story much the same as that of the City of a Thousand Stories—a great ruler of the past had gone into the Forever Desert and left behind a treasure, within which was the truth of their city's history. For generations since, brave explorers had left the city in search of that treasure, yet none had returned.

"I am the first in fifty years," she boasted. "And I mean to be the last."

"How so?" Ethike asked.

She claimed to have found previously untold stories, ones that made it clear to her that previous Tombseekers had been searching in the wrong direction. The stories she'd discovered were not about the city's great ruler, but about an obscure and forgotten historical figure. A figure named . . .

"Osi," Ethike signed.

Her cheeks widened into the most beautiful smile Ethike had ever seen. At the same time, tears collected on the sills of her eyes, nearly spilling before she wiped them away with the back of a finger.

"You are the first to understand," she signed, looking away to compose herself. "You must know how I feel."

Ethike reached across the table and took her hand in his. It wasn't something he had ever done before, but it felt right in the moment True.

"I am Ogisi Ethike," he signed.

"Ogisi Silah," she signed with a small laugh.

In that laugh, in the brief moment her mouth was open, Ethike thought he saw something strange. Only later in the conversation, when she laughed again, did he confirm that the rough stump of pink in the back of her throat was the jagged remnant of a severed tongue.

5

IN THE HISTORIES, A severed tongue could mean many things. Sometimes, it was the punishment for an escaped criminal. Sometimes, it was the badge of an elite fighter, sworn to forever keep the secrets to their martial prowess. Some histories even told of whole cities with their tongues cut out, as a sacrifice to the Goddess.

It wasn't just Ogisi Silah. Nor just her companions. Everyone in the lodge, patrons and staff alike, at some point opened their mouths to reveal a stump of tongue. Ethike did not understand what their lack of tongues meant any more than he understood their infantile ears. But he was an ogisi. His purpose was to lay the bricks of the bridge between unknown and known. He was called to take the risk of learning that which might change his understanding of the world.

He was about to ask why they had no tongues when Aza tapped him on the shoulder. "We must rest for tomorrow," she signed, her eyes firmly on Silah and her compatriots.

Ethike regarded Silah with a regretful smile. "Hope to see you again," he signed, then added a nod for her companions.

She smiled back. "I hope you will too," she signed.

By the time Ethike and Aza reached the room Zogo had rented them, the merchant was asleep on one of the thin beds. Aza lay down beside the door and fell into her half sleep, with shallow breathing that hinted she was more awake than she appeared. Ethike sat on the room's other bed, turning the puzzle of the tongues and ears over and over for hours.

He thought about Silah as well. Nothing in particular, just the fact of her existence. There was another city in the Forever Desert, with ogisi of their own. And some of those ogisi also sought out Osi's Tomb—a simple fact that spawned endless questions. Were these other cities that Osi had traveled to? Or perhaps other cities that had been ruled by Obasa? Did their ogisi work in Great Temples? Did their people enjoy eating bread?

He didn't realize he'd fallen asleep, but by the time he woke up, the heat of the day had passed and it was time to continue their journey. He was excited for what other interesting characters the Forever Desert might hold.

Outside, Silah and her team were waiting.

"Ogisi Ethike," she signed with warm familiarity. "The Goddess has brought us together again."

"It seems so," he signed back.

Zogo strode into view, blocking Ethike from Silah. "Wagon is ready, Bookboy. No time for chat-chat."

The other ogisi waited until Zogo had moved on before signing. "This desert is no place to travel alone." She smiled.

Then Aza appeared beside Ethike, stone in her demeanor. "You are hardly alone," she responded, then gestured to Silah's companions.

"Not all company is created equal," Silah replied, revealing again her blunted tongue as she laughed.

They do not trust her . . . Ethike thought. He appreciated Zogo's and Aza's protectiveness of him, but it was clear that its roots grew from the kind of xenophobia common in the city. All people knew about the Forever Desert was that it was home to the Ajungo and other terrifying evils. A place so dangerous even Obasa the Wise had not survived it. Aza was a soldier, trained in the art of wariness, and Zogo clearly had his own history with the desert that had soured him on it.

But Silah was an interesting person and a fellow ogisi. If he couldn't trust her, who could he trust?

Trust is the only coin that doubles when spent. Spend generously.

"We do not have space in the wagon for all of you," Ethike signed. "But if you want to ride beside us, we welcome you."

Aza left to climb into the passenger side of the driver's seat. Zogo joined her, but not before he leveled a look at Ethike that was equal parts disbelief and disgust.

Silah and her two companions rode together on camelback. On one side of her was a towering but lean man who wore the same muted glower as Aza's—no doubt a soldier. On the other side was a proud-faced man nearly drowning in his red silks—clearly a wealthy merchant.

Despite Zogo's and Aza's apprehensions, Silah and her group made for easy travel companions. During the night rides, they kept to themselves. Even during short breaks, they maintained their distance while they ate and drank. Only when they were done traveling for the day, when the sun was creeping toward its zenith and they all sought shelter in the shade of a tall dune, did they join Ethike's party in full.

Together, the six of them shared a meal. Afterward, Zogo enjoyed puffs from his pipe while the soldiers and the red-silked man lay down to rest. Ethike finally had time to speak with Silah alone. He slid over toward her, trying to find the most appropriate way to ask the questions on his mind.

"Where are your tongues?" he signed.

Silah laughed. She was so joyful when she laughed, all cheeks and glow. "I suspect the same place as your ears," she signed back.

When Ethike frowned, she only laughed harder. "There is no drink so refreshing as your confusion, Ogisi Ethike. Do you not know the history?"

He realized how unsophisticated he must have seemed—she appeared to know things about the City of a Thousand Stories, but he knew nothing about where she was from.

"Tell me," he signed. "Please."

Silah's eyes twinkled—there were no sweeter words to an ogisi than a request for explanation.

"When Obasa the Wise first left the safety of our city and went deep into the Forever Desert," she began, with all the expected polish of one who has told the same story dozens of times, "he came upon a child standing alone on the sand. Though he had to continue on his journey, he sent one of his servants to question the boy and provide him with water. Strangely, the servant returned at the end of the day, hours later than expected.

"'What slowed your return?' one of the guards asked.

"'What slowed your return?' the servant responded.

"'What do you mean?' the guard asked.

"'What do you mean?' the servant responded.

"The servant did nothing but repeat the guard's words, and it soon became so strange that the other members of Obasa's expedition joined the discussion with their own questions. The servant's head whipped this way and that, repeating every word each of them said. This went on for a time before the first guard suddenly collapsed. Blood poured forth from his mouth, and no attempts to heal him succeeded. Obasa saw the commotion and went over to investigate, where he found the servant continuing to repeat each person's words.

"As he watched the chaos ensue and more of his companions collapse in bloody heaps, Obasa came to understand what was happening. Whatever beast had indwelled the servant was traveling from person to person, host to host, and could only be defeated by removing its greatest weapon—words. Thus, he drew a knife, took ahold of his tongue, and cut it away. Soon, each member of his party died until it was just he and the servant. The servant looked at him the way a caged lion looks at raw meat, then strode off into the desert."

Ethike had heard the story a thousand times before.

Yet this version was completely wrong. Utterly without evidence, unfounded in any of the histories from any of the Great Temples.

"So, you see," Silah continued, "there remains a beast in the Forever Desert who makes a weapon of words. And this"—she opened her mouth and pointed to the stump of her tongue—"is how we protect ourselves." She finished with an incline of her head and a flourish of her hands.

Ethike waved his hands in applause, but he was filled with discomfort and doubt. Surely, if such an outlandish story of Obasa existed anywhere, he would have heard of it.

Right?

It was the third Memento of the Ogisi that cured him of his uncertainty.

Even water has a story.

It was the ogisi's job to debate stories, yes. To research them and verify them. But, most of all, to *share* them. In hopes that the sharing of stories could resolve what no amount of debate could.

So Ethike shared.

"In our city, we have a similar story," he signed, drawing everyone's attention. "About a creature with the most beautiful voice who lures travelers into its embrace and steals their spirit from them until all that remains is a frail body, devoid of any connection to the Goddess. Not a beast that is dangerous to speak to, but a beast dangerous to listen to. This is why"—he raised his hands to the cauterized flesh of his ears, tapping them—"we all join the Silence."

Silah seemed to digest that for a moment before regarding Ethike with a shrug and smile.

"What do you call this beast of yours?" Silah asked.

Zogo motioned for Ethike to give no response, but Ethike shook his head and smiled apologetically. Even after a full day traveling together, the merchant still didn't trust her.

"The Ajungo," Ethike signed.

Silah nodded knowingly, her eyes alight. "Different stories," she signed. "Same name."

6

THE TWO PARTIES BECAME more intermingled after that. The red-silked man took to sitting beside Zogo in the wagon's driver's seat, while Aza took the open camel as her own, traveling beside Silah's unusually tall guard.

Which left Ethike and Silah riding together in the wagon. Ethike could not imagine a better travel partner. Silah possessed a capacious mind, and he found great pleasure in wandering down its corridors and running his fingers along its shelves. There were some histories she was unfamiliar with, but there were many more she knew that Ethike had never heard—even stories about Osi. Osi and the Red Child. Osi and the Broken Tower. Osi and the Mask of a Thousand Faces. Ethike had scavenged for years to find even the smallest crumbs about the man who may have been "the last Truthseeker," yet within minutes of speaking with Silah, he had been given a feast.

"Surely you have heard the story of Osi's Lover?" Silah asked. It was just the two of them, Zogo and Aza driving on the other side of the wagon cabin's wall.

"Osi had no lover," Ethike shot back. He could accept there were some histories about Osi he had not heard, but he could not imagine that such a defining fact was entirely missing from all the books in the Great Temple.

"He did," Silah signed. "Her name is not known, but she is described as so wise and powerful that she learned to live without sleep. Sometimes, she would spend the night buried in her books. Sometimes, she would spend the night buried in bed with Osi . . ."

"Is that so . . ." Ethike signed, flabbergasted. "What happened to her? I thought Osi died alone."

"He killed her," Silah signed, then let her hands fall with a satisfied smile that said she knew Ethike wouldn't be able to resist asking for more.

"Impossible."

"While he was away in the Broken Tower, she had fallen under the spell of a powerful king who promised her ten goats and a hundred chickens if—"

The wagon jolted to a halt and Silah's hands stilled, her eyes widening.

"Shouting," she signed.

She moved to the back of the wagon, but he grabbed her arm.

"Are you sure?" he asked, staring at her hard. "Not singing?"

She rolled her eyes and leapt out through the back door, onto the sand. He followed immediately after. Maybe she didn't believe his city's story about the Ajungo, but he cared about her enough that he couldn't just let her hurry to her doom.

He rounded the wagon to find two lizards scuttling down a nearby dune. Their backs were covered in dozens of overlapping rings of soft flesh, and a small mound jutted out the end of their snouts. They were each as long as Ethike was tall, but they must have been babies by the way they waddled and by their jovial, helpless demeanor.

They were known as bagobas. Incredible creatures. Ethike had seen diagrams and descriptions of them in the Great Temple of Onfe. They were rare lizards, in part because they mostly lived underground and in part because they needed so much water they often died of dehydration well before adulthood. Ethike was grateful to see such magnificent creatures in person, though he wondered why two babies were out wandering alone, far from any water source.

His question was answered immediately. The ground shivered beneath them. The sand ahead of the wagon erupted into the air and fell in a rain of hot grains that became cool, dark soil. In the aftermath of the sand-and-soil shower, a creature emerged from the earth. It was a replica of the two babies that had waddled past moments before, only ten times the size. The ringed flesh on its back was hard armor, the fleshy mound on the end of its snout a curved and pointed horn large enough to skewer their wagon.

Beneath the massive bagoba, bubbling up from the hole the animal had created, was water.

Ethike stared in wonder at the surging spring as the lizard opened its monstrous maw, a cave of off-ivory stalagmites and stalactites—jagged, misshapen things slathered in saliva. It was so far away that Ethike didn't consider whether it would attack anyone. How could it?

Its giant legs covered the distance to the wagon in a few steps. Then its jaws were closing upon them.

*   *   *

Teeth snapping together. A spray of innards and hot air. Camels chomped into ribbons of blood and flesh. Ethike was caught in the afterblow—a thousand tiny hands of wetness slapped him all over, blinding him in gore.

He rubbed his forearm across his face, clearing his eyes to witness the battle erupting before him.

Aza, bound in iridescent scales of light that shone through her black silks, was descending through the air toward the bagoba. Silah's guard was similarly engulfed in light, but he was on the ground, attacking the lizard from behind.

Ethike had never seen the Seeing Arts used for fighting. Within the city walls, where there was nothing to fight, Sight was used exclusively by people hoping to entertain or educate themselves with visions of the past. Aza's superhuman leap was impressive, but he couldn't imagine how a power intended for history lessons could be used to defeat monsters twenty times a Seer's size. Even as the two warriors surrounded the bagoba, the animal was already reacting, sweeping its heavy, spiked tail directly at Silah's companion. Horror swelled within Ethike as the tail tore closer and closer to collision with the man's body.

Yet when the bagoba's heavy, spiked tail struck the man, he was unmoved. Instead of being batted across the desert, Silah's soldier stood like a struck bell, the light within his skin rippling from the impact. Then he reared back an arm and plunged it into the bagoba's tail, burying up to his shoulder in its meat. The animal's mouth opened and released a vibration that was cut short when Aza crashed her feet down onto its snout, slamming its mouth closed with such force that the large fangs of the bottom jaw exploded through the upper, blasting through skin and muscle and nostrils.

Ethike had always thought he knew what fear looked like, but as he saw the spirit of the bagoba collapse into itself, he understood it anew. Fear makes big things small, makes small things disappear. And so Ethike watched the bagoba's spirit shrink before his eyes, the mighty beast reduced to something akin to an abused child, huddling and hiding before a violent ire.

Then, with the lizard's tail still pinned down by Silah's guardsman, Aza grabbed the beast's horn and twisted it as if it were cloth—or hair, or anything but the bone that it was—until it broke off at the base. She raised the horn above her head and drove it down between the bagoba's eyes.

The beast dropped, silent as stone. Red lines trickled down the gray skin of its pulverized skull.

Silah's guardsman strode calmly away, shaking the blood and bits from his arm. Zogo tossed a handkerchief to Aza, who wiped the gore from her body.

In the chaos of the fighting, Ethike had forgotten about the babies. He saw them now, peeking out over the top of a distant dune. Before, they had walked near the party so comfortably. Now, they knew better. Bagobas were feared and ancient creatures, featured in many of the oldest histories of the Forever Desert. Ethike wondered how old their mother had been, how many dry desert summers she had survived, how many battles she had emerged from victorious. All for it to end simply because her children were ignorant of a story she had already learned—humans were beasts to be feared.

Even gardens have an end.

Zogo smacked Ethike's shoulder. "Are ya alive, Bookboy?" he asked as he surveyed the splattered remains of their camels and the surging spring of water ahead of them. "Do ya have water? Find joy in these things and fix your face."

None of them appeared troubled by what they had witnessed. The two soldiers were already off-loading supplies from the wagon. Silah was checking her own supplies. Zogo was signing back and forth with the red-silked man, recounting their experiences of the battle.

Ethike saw no evidence that any of them felt as he did. Poisoned. Covered in filth. His insides jumbled up and flipped over and spun around. He had seen a side of Aza, of humanity in general, that he hadn't known before. There was plenty of war and violence in the histories, but those stories didn't smell like iron and death. They didn't force him to turn his eyes away from a seemingly endless fount of blood slapping out onto the sand.

But Zogo was right. They were alive. They had water. Maybe this was the only way.

Ethike tried to find joy in that.

7

BOTH OF ETHIKE'S CAMELS had died in the attack. Of Silah's, two had fled during the fighting, and the remaining one was trained for war, not pulling loads. Which meant they would have to leave the wagon—and most of their supplies—behind.

There was division over whether to continue. Zogo and Silah wanted to press forward. The others wanted to end the journey and return home.

Again, it seemed to come down to Ethike's decision. There was sense in returning to the city and resupplying. But the only treasure he sought at Osi's Tomb was the story of the city's origins, and they didn't need a wagon to carry that.

Also, in the quiet folds of his heart, he didn't think he could endure the shame of returning to the city empty-handed. All those people had been there to see him off. They'd looked at him as a hero, and he felt an obligation to honor that. And then there was Uwi. She would be happy to see him, but what sort of example would he be setting for her? To quit when things were difficult? To depend on the comforts of home at the first sign of fear? He'd already been gone for two weeks. He wouldn't be able to look her in the eyes if those two weeks away from her were for nothing.

"We have encountered misfortune," he signed for them all to see, "but when future ogisi tell of this journey, that misfortune will make the story all the sweeter."

Even water has a story.

"Let's continue," he finished.

Silah was gracious enough to let them use her camel for pack space, so they took what supplies they could carry from the wagon and continued on foot. By Ethike's estimations, they were roughly a few weeks' ride from Osi's Tomb. But three weeks on camelback would be three months on foot. Moreover, they had no wagon cover to protect them from the sun, no drums of water to replenish their skins.

He marked their location on his map, so that, if the situation became dire, they could find their way back.

That first week, Ethike learned that walking through the desert was considerably more difficult than riding through it. He hadn't realized just how deep the sand was, how much it latched onto his ankles like a rambunctious child. Sand found its way into every part of him, even beneath his clothes. It didn't help that, since they had to ration water, they were no longer able to bathe. Instead, they took to what Zogo had called "dry-washing," where they rubbed a handful of sand against themselves as if it were soap. It did nothing for their smell, nor did it relieve Ethike of the sticky feeling of sweat that clung to him by the end of the day.

The second week was no better. The only difference was that Zogo began telling stories to pass the time and distract Ethike from his visible discomfort. Not the histories from the Great Temples, but folktales passed among the citizens of the city—unfounded in any books, derived from one person's peerings into history.

"The Three Snakes," Zogo signed, "battled such creatures often. That's where the sand comes from. When men fight, bones are broken. But when beasts fight, bones *explode*. It's all bits of bone, the sand is. Bet ya didn't know that story, did ya Bookboy?"

Ethike wanted to accept the story as it was—*even water has a story,* after all—but he couldn't help asking questions. "Do you really believe that, Zogo?"

Zogo scoffed. "If I can't eat it or spend it, I don't believe in it," he signed. "That's the difference between ya ebony tower types and the rest of us. We don't know if our stories are true, and we don't care. But ya ogisi actually believe what ya see."

"Read," Ethike countered.

"Wha?"

"We don't See the histories, we read them. They are written."

Zogo gave Ethike a withering look. "And ya read with ya ass, do ya?"

Ethike didn't respond.

The third week, a wagon appeared on the horizon. A shadow atop a dune, backdropped by the orange disc of the ascending sun.

Ethike froze, but Aza's hands flashed high above her head for all of them behind her to see.

"Keep moving!"

As so they did. The team's mood shifted from tired optimism to fearful urgency. Ethike saw the same mistrust he'd seen all along the journey—from mistrusting him to mistrusting Silah and her companions. Each time, however, that mistrust had proven misplaced. All the stories of the Forever Desert said it was full of horrible things, but so far he had only found friends and a protective mother bagoba. The wagon had maintained a respectful, parallel path. No sign of danger.

Trust is the only coin that doubles when spent.

"Be at ease," he signed to the party. "They are like us, peaceful travelers."

Then it began to move closer.

Its pace didn't change, but just a slight shift in angle was enough to shorten the distance from a full horizon away to half. By the time the sun was nearing noon and they were supposed to camp for the day, the wagon was even closer.

Luckily, the wagon riders also stopped to set up camp for the day. Ethike watched them angle their camels down to the base of a distant dune, then dismount.

"Good," Zogo signed, squinting to peer further ahead. "If they stop, we continue. We can escape those dung beetles."

Ethike looked around at both his team and Silah's. They hid their exhaustion better than he did, but it was still clear in the gaunt angles of their faces. His own body was beginning to fail him—he had a persistent itch in his eye that he had never experienced before, one that seemed to demand a salve of moisture rather than a scratch.

They all needed rest.

"We'll stop there," he signed, nodding toward a patch of shade at the bottom of the dune ahead of them. "These people have not shown themselves to be enemies. We cannot treat them as if they are."

He still felt weighed down by what they had done to the bagoba. Moving through the world full of fear and mistrust, killing anything unfamiliar . . . that was no way to live. There had to be an end to it.

Even gardens have an end.

He didn't fully understand the Three Mementos—their origins and meaning were lost to history, the subject of persistent debate among ogisi. But they seemed to apply to every situation, bringing him comfort when he most needed it.

"A godsblind fool ya are, Bookboy," Zogo signed, trudging through the sand toward him. "Ya think ya know this desert, eh? I've been a decade wandering these sands. I've seen cruelness ya brainless self cannot imagine. I know these people—they are beasts behind man-shaped masks. When whoever drives that wagon gets here, they will disembowel your soft flesh and mount ya for the vultures."

From the way Zogo's hands shook, and the viciousness of his words, it would be reasonable to assume he was angry. But Ethike could only see how scared he was. Not just in that moment, but always. He hid it in so many ways—caution or overconfidence, disinterest or anger, a cold stare or a warm story—but, now that he knew to look, Ethike could see that the fear was always there.

On one thing, however, Zogo was right: Ethike could not imagine the horrors he must have encountered in his travels. Nor the nightmares Aza, whose wary stare said she agreed with Zogo, had fought. They were all more experienced in the dangers of the world than he, and it was from those experiences their fear grew.

But memories from the past need not poison trust in the future.

"I understand your words, Zogo," Ethike signed. "And I trust your counsel."

Zogo sighed with such relief that Ethike winced. He knew his next words would betray the man's newfound comfort.

"But we will rest here. Silah may do as she wishes with her team, of course."

Silah stared into Ethike, and he accepted her gaze and all its questioning. Eventually she smiled and looked away. "For better or worse, I trust you. We will stay."

Ethike nodded. "Aza, keep watch. When the wagon reaches us, we will welcome them as fellow travelers. As friends."

He was surprised at how steady his signing was. How confident he appeared. He wished he felt that way, but Zogo's plea had not gone unfelt. Their fate was in his hands—he'd just as likely killed them as saved them.

As they set up camp, Zogo walked a short distance away and smoked his pipe. When he returned, his cheeks streaked with tracks of tears, he lay down on his sleep mat and closed his eyes. The rest of them did the same.

By the time they woke, the wagon was upon them.

*   *   *

Aza's hand shook Ethike awake.

"They're here," she signed.

It was full night, black but for the moon's cold yellow face. Ethike watched the wagon descend toward them, leaving parallel gouges in the sand.

Though not directly toward them. The wagon was moving down its dune along the side, not quite toward Ethike and his companions. By the time it arrived beside them at the bottom of the dune, it was roughly a dozen paces away. Ethike watched in confusion as the wagon churned past without acknowledging them at all.

"What is this?" he signed, mostly to himself.

From the front seat of the wagon, a driver suddenly turned to face him. She appeared slightly older than Ethike, likely in her forties, and was shrouded in white silks. Her hair spilled out from beneath her head wrap; a trio of gold chains dangled between her nose and lips.

Her eyes were shut.

Not eyelids-clasped-together shut, but sewn shut; loops of thread stitched top and bottom into one. Two other women, sitting in the back of the wagon, were the same. In silence and bewilderment, Ethike and his party watched the wagon continue up the next dune and out of sight.

Three blind women, traveling together through the Forever Desert, riding obliviously past a party with trained soldiers. Surely they had known, when leaving wherever they were from, the risk they were taking. Ethike wondered what it was that could have pushed them into the desert. Perhaps they were merchants, off to meet a trade partner. Or perhaps they were fighters, on their way to the next battle.

Ethike knew, though, that neither of those were the case. He could recognize ogisi as readily as he could recognize his own reflection. Like himself and Silah, they had their own story about the Ajungo, one that demanded they sacrifice their eyes. Also like himself and Silah, they had discovered the truth of Osi's Tomb.

And they were going to beat him to it.

8

ETHIKE HAD BELIEVED THE Forever Desert to be like a city: an environment shaped by the collective will of those who called it home. Instead, the desert was a place with a will of its own, with its own unspoken desires and muted machinations. For centuries it had hidden the truth of Osi's Tomb, then revealed it all at once. It was as if all of them—himself, Silah, the wagon riders, and who knew how many others—were caught in a pull of the desert's design, lured by its song.

The weeks passed like a hot wind. For a while, they continued to see wagon tracks ahead of them, but soon even those disappeared as the gap between themselves and the mysterious wagon grew. They were forced to further ration water and steps alike, minimize their exposure to the sun. Each of them shed weight, their cheeks concaved, their eyes bulged from receded depths. Ethike stayed mostly in his thoughts, and most of his thoughts were of Uwi. He tried to imagine what her days were like—when she got up and who her friends were at school and how much she was enjoying her new life at the Capitol, mingling with the children of the city's elite. During the day, just before he went to bed, he'd say a prayer to the Goddess, asking Her to ensure that Uwi felt his love no matter how far away he was.

When he wasn't thinking about Uwi, he worried that all their traveling was a waste. The blind ogisi in the wagon would soon reach Osi's Tomb. And even if they somehow got delayed, what if Ethike's story about the Ajungo was wrong? What if having a tongue—or eyes—meant certain death?

But his faith kept him going. His faith in his research, his faith in his companions, his faith in Osi. Rather than letting his thoughts dwell on their misfortune, he recited the Three Mementos. Hour after hour, day after day, week after week, those ancient words filled him with hope and purpose.

Even deserts have a beginning.

Even gardens have an end.

Even water has a story.

He recited them to himself through midday heat and nighttime chill, his gaze locked on the sand before him.

Until, suddenly, it was not just sand that sat before him.

A black dot on the horizon became a vague and hazy smear. A vague and hazy smear became spear shafts embedded thickly into the landscape. Embedded spear shafts became tightly packed trees with trunks that were intent on carving up the sky, striking so high that Ethike couldn't find their tops. Trees that dwarfed mountains, with trunks, branches, and leaves a black that was deeper than any other, that seemed to suck in light and destroy it, howling in defiance of the desert's burning gold.

Ethike's heartbeat tripled, each pound a fist into the chest. This was it.

Suddenly, something soft but weighty crashed into him, wrapped around him, squeezed him tight. It was Silah, her arms cloaked over his shoulders, her cheek and his conjoined.

"Ethike, we are here," she signed in front of his face. "Obasa and the Mourning Tree!"

Obasa and the Mourning Tree was an obscure story. In it, Obasa finds an oasis deep in the Forever Desert, only to drown in its waters, ascend into the clouds, and rain down on the land so hard that a tree grows out of the sand. To most ogisi, it was purely symbolic, not an actual historical account. Yet it was the only one, outside stories of the Ajungo, that mentioned Obasa's death. And when Ethike had compared it to stories of Osi falling asleep beneath a great tree, he'd found the connection too strong to ignore.

"Osi's Descendants will be here," Silah signed, motioning at the settlement. "The guardians of the tomb."

Ethike didn't know such a story, but he had full trust in Silah's knowledge.

"We are here," he signed, and tears immediately brimmed in his eyes.

Ethike had always expected a mediocre life. He knew he was not called to greatness, nor did he seek it. Yet somehow he'd become the first ogisi from the City of a Thousand Stories ever to lay eyes on Osi's Tomb. Even if the wagon had arrived before him and all of

Osi's treasure was taken, he'd still accomplished something worthy of legend, something sure to earn more than a few books written about him when he returned.

It was for that reason he cried. Because he was grateful to see what stood before him, grateful that his life had given him more than he'd ever asked for.

Though the trees dominated the horizon, it was another week of travel before the party actually reached them. As the distance closed, the trees grew in size from large to incomprehensible, and Ethike had to keep his gaze down to avoid the dizzying feeling.

That was how he saw the settlement. Nestled at the foot of the trees, a tiny thing. It seemed birthed from the desert itself, gold sand raised and molded into homes and inns and markets.

Silah tapped him, face bright with a smile. "You ready?"

They descended into the settlement.

Two sorts of people trekked back and forth across a spacious plaza. The first walked with a calm ease, clad in either red or white igbulu, their chins up, their mouths in static half smiles. The ones in white had their eyelids sewn shut like the wagon riders from earlier, while those in red—judging by their full ears and signed discussions—were like Silah—missing tongues.

All of them ogisi.

Following behind each ogisi was the settlement's second sort of person. They were shorter, with cracked, splotched skin and the downcast, shuffling gait of a body carrying more weight than it ought to. Yet they carried no load that Ethike could see; even their clothes—thin brown robes with holes eaten through them—were too meager to be of any burden. The only thing weighing them down was a strange necklace, a thick chain dangling over their shoulders, each end of it capped by a black, rotted hand.

The necklaces were so painfully real that Ethike thought he could smell the dead flesh, the foulest odor he had ever encountered. It snaked itself into the back of his throat and forced out of him a wretched, gut-churning heave. With how dehydrated he was, his vomit came out in sticky globs, slapping against his open palm and sliding through his fingers onto the ground. When he finally unfolded himself, he saw some of the settlement's ogisi watching him as they continued on their ways, faces blank.

The others—the short, burdened people—didn't look to him at all. They kept their gazes down, backs hunched. Each of their arms ended in a round, raw stump.

Silah approached him, her nose buried in the crook of her elbow. "This cannot be," she signed, shaking her head. "This foul place cannot be Osi's Tomb."

A man emerged from the town on a single intent line toward Ethike and his party as the settlement's inhabitants crisscrossed around him. He was in his later years, with two white tufts of hair by his temples and a face crinkled by time. He strode with a tinge of regality that was beyond even that of the settlement's ogisi. Three handless people followed behind him.

His igbulu was black, and his ears were two bubbled walls of scorched flesh.

Like back home.

"I am called the Aleke," he signed, his eyes taking each of them in. "Welcome to my city. And to the rest of your lives."

9

THE ALEKE'S THRONE ROOM was a sun-drenched terrace on the roof of the closest thing to a palace the settlement had. At the center, flanked on either side by rows of potted palms and a dozen of the handless people, the Aleke seated himself on a wooden throne.

Ethike had read that word before: Aleke. It was an old word that roughly translated to "king of the land." But it was very specific, a title used by farmers to describe not their dominion of the land, but their ability to nurture it. A hundred strides to their left were trees that each rivaled a city in size. Were those what had earned this "Aleke" his title?

The Aleke ordered his handless servants to bring over wicker chairs for Ethike and the others to sit. Other handless servants brought them platters of fruit and meat. Of all the things he had seen since leaving the city, it was this that struck him as the strangest—people with able hands forcing those without to wait on them.

"Thank you," Ethike said to a passing servant, who momentarily raised his head. The servant's mouth opened and closed in an odd way before he thrust his gaze back down and continued on his way.

The Aleke raised his arms high and rolled his wrists in the air to get everyone's attention. "You are here for Osi's Tomb," he signed.

"Yes," Ethike signed. "But we saw another wagon ahead of us. Are we too late?"

The Aleke smiled. "For the treasure? Yes, you are far too late. But is it the treasure you came for?" He drank back the last of his palm wine and motioned for a handless servant to refill it. "Or the truth?"

"The truth," Ethike signed back immediately. Zogo flinched beside him.

"Ah." The Aleke's smile deepened. "I never get tired of telling this. Here it is: I am an ogisi, like the two of you."

They all were, he explained. Every person in the settlement was an ogisi from a city of the Forever Desert. Each of them had discovered the truth of Osi's Tomb and arrived at the same place. It had become so common that over time, a settlement was built to welcome the new ogisi.

"I call it the City of Truth," he signed, then spread his arms and grin wide.

The Aleke had been there for decades, but even he didn't know how long ago the first ogisi had arrived. He'd received the title of Aleke from the previous holder, who had received it from the one before. There was no record of anyone ever finding Osi's Tomb. No record of treasure. No record of the truth of any city's origins.

"Then perhaps we have come to the wrong place," Ethike signed. It seemed more likely that they were simply incorrect about the location of the Tomb than all the histories being a farce.

"Ah." The Aleke's eyes twinkled and he leaned forward as if his next words were conspiracy. "But there are records—many, many records—of one thing. A beast who sings such poison that it is better to cut away your ears than listen to it. Who is so hungry for words it is better to cut away your tongue than converse with it. Whose image is so terrible it is better to cut out your eyes than look upon it.

"The Ajungo."

The City of Truth had a library, maintained by the ogisi over generations, and the oldest texts all agreed that the Ajungo lived within the ring of trees. This was where Osi's journey had ended. Whether there was treasure was unknown. Whether the city's origins were trapped in a buried gourd was unknown. All that was known—truly known—was that the Ajungo remained within those trees, waiting.

"For what?" Ethike asked.

The Aleke shrugged. "The records don't answer that. The only ones who would know are the fish." He motioned to the servants. "They come from the trees, where the Ajungo is. They've been there since long before any of us ogisi arrived. They're mostly docile, but they fight like hell if we try to enter their home. So we've trained them to serve, and they've done so since. You can have one if you'd like."

Ethike looked around the room at the servants, unable to keep the confusion from his face. There was nothing fishlike about them—they looked like ordinary humans. Of slighter build than usual, and their skin seemed in poor health, but humans nonetheless. He didn't understand.

"Can we ask them?" Ethike asked.

"How would they answer?" the Aleke replied. "Fish can't talk. Even if they had hands, they can't learn language, the dim beasts." He closed his eyes and took a deep, satisfied breath, as if invigorated by his own storytelling. "So now you know the final, glorious truth of Osi's Tomb: It is a fool's quest, handed down for centuries to be taken up by each subsequent generation of fools. Those who seek the truth have no way to find it and those who know the truth have no way to share it." He clapped his hands together and leaned back with a smile. "Is this life not beautiful?"

So that was it. If the Aleke was to be believed, all those stories Ethike had devoted his life to studying, all those books he'd read, were little better than the stories in Zogo's head. Their journey had reached its end.

Even gardens have an end.

Suddenly, the rooftop glowed as Zogo and Aza sparkled with light, as did Silah's companions. The Aleke had presented his truth, but they sought their own.

For the first time, Ethike understood why they used Sight. He felt the urge himself. When the stories one is told conflict with the world one knows, what other choice is there but to seek out other stories? Stories that could make sense of a senseless world.

Silah's hand fell on his thigh. He looked over and her face was a conclusion: It was over.

The Aleke finished his second glass and motioned for a third. One of the servant men brought over a pitcher, but tripped and landed hard on the brick floor, crushing the pitcher into a mound of glass shards and soaking the terrace with the sharp scent of palm wine.

Immediately, the Aleke's skin leapt with light, an armor of iridescent scales enveloping him. Before the handless man could rise, the Aleke snatched a serving platter and flung it at him. In his drunkenness, the Aleke missed. The platter sailed high and struck a different servant. Powered by Sight, the platter sheared through the servant's forehead, slicing through skull and brain before lodging firmly in the top of the spine.

The blow was no doubt immediately fatal, but the man clung to life. He stood upright and proud as his blood poured down the remains of his face. His mouth opened and closed, opened and closed, over and over, changing shapes each time.

Then half of his head fell away and his life was ended.

All around, the mouths of the servants began opening and closing and changing shape in the same manner. Two of them scooped the man's body up and dragged it away, as if it were routine. All the while, their mouths moved, and Ethike could see how, from a certain perspective, it would look like they were singing.

"See why we call them fish?" the Aleke signed. He appeared to have already forgotten about the servants—both the one he killed and the one who had actually spilled the wine. "Big, dumb, clumsy fish. That's why I keep their hands cut, so they don't hurt anyone. Feels like a compliment, to be honest." He raised his glass and another handless servant rushed to fill it. "At least you can eat fish."

* * *

In the days that followed, Ethike kept to himself. He left the Aleke's palace first thing each morning, before the others woke. He walked about the City of Truth, observed, and recorded what he saw. He ignored everyone, even Zogo and Aza. Even Silah.

But not the servants. In the evenings, when they brought his food, he tried to talk to them, but it proved impossible. He learned that those mouth shapes were their language. They communicated in sounds, which he could not hear. And he communicated with his hands, which they could not understand.

In his exploration of the settlement, he watched the other ogisi. They lived enviable lives—dining and reading, watching plays or listening to music, watching their children grow and play and having them home by sundown to enjoy the rare treasure of peaceful domesticity. It was unclear to him whether the Aleke would let any of them leave, but he supposed it didn't matter. The Tombseekers were all like him—lonely, desperate, in search of something to define themselves by. All that awaited them back home was the scorn and humiliation of failure. Here, they were the heroes they'd always believed themselves to be.

If it weren't for Uwi, perhaps he would have felt the same.

No.

There were also the people from the trees.

Every time one of the handless servants brought Ethike his food, their own rotted hands dangling at their chest, he wanted to weep for them. He had devoted his life to becoming ogisi. Being ogisi was all he knew. Yet it was clear to him that this was the inevitable end point of the ogisi's mission. None of the settlement's residents appeared bothered that their lives were built upon a foundation of suffering, and he knew that if he spent enough time in the City of Truth, then he would grow as accustomed to that suffering as he had to the stench of rotting hands. He too would soon fail to see humanity in these people. Losing sight of others' humanity was the seed from which all cruelty grew.

It was for that reason, and for Uwi, that he decided to leave the City of Truth.

Both Aza and Zogo declined to return. Aza because she wanted to spend more time exploring the desert. Zogo because he claimed the Elders had sent him on this quest to get rid of him anyway—"they'll only suffer a man like me so long."

"And go where?" Silah asked when he told her. It had been three days since they last spoke, and he'd forgotten how much he enjoyed her presence. It was just the two of them, standing in her room across from each other.

"Home," Ethike replied. "I have to return to Uwi."

She nodded but said nothing else. In the stillness of her fingers, he understood.

He briefly considered asking Silah to come back with him. More than considered. Desired. He wanted her to return with him. Yet, despite how easy it typically was for him to speak his heart, he found it hard to communicate what was inside him, and he let the conversation—and their travels together—come to an end.

Even gardens have an end.

It didn't take him long to pack his things, take a camel, and slip out of the settlement. The only guards were positioned around the giant trees, strangely, so he wasn't stopped or even noticed. His plan was to ride back to their discarded wagon first, where hopefully the supplies they'd left behind hadn't been picked clean. From there, it was on to the city. Though he hadn't found the truth he'd hoped for, he'd found the truth that needed to be told.

Maybe it would be the end of the ogisi altogether.

Maybe it would be the beginning of something better.

Even deserts have a beginning.

On his way out of the Aleke's palace, he saw a small troupe of the handless servants carrying something between them. It was long and draped in pale cloth, heavy enough to require several strong shoulders to hold it aloft. They were proceeding in a slow march, tears burrowing down their cheeks, shoulders shaking from sobs. Ethike decided that it must have been a human body, and spots of red where blood had seeped through the cloth confirmed his suspicion. He wondered whether it was the body of the servant who had been killed. Perhaps this was his funeral. Ethike would never know, though. He would never know who that man was or where he'd come from or where he'd planned to go. Sadly, that was the fate of most stories—they died with the holder.

He watched them take the body into the ring of enormous trees and then they were gone.

It took most of the day just to climb out from the basin the City of Truth sat in. By the time he reached the top of a dune with a view of the whole settlement, the sun was high on its throne. People and buildings and wells, all so small beside the trees that aspired to the heavens. In his observations of the city, the trees were the thing he had learned least about. They were a mystery, not just in their size, but in their very existence: How much water would such trees need to survive? And where, in an endless and unforgiving desert, were they getting it?

Ethike was taking his final glance back at the city, ready to begin his trek home, when the desert began to move. It started beneath his feet, the sand sliding slowly out from under his surefooted camel and down toward the city. Then it began to twist into itself as sand vortexed in from all directions, converging on a point hundreds of strides to the west of the settlement. There was a small hole there, not much larger than a person, and it appeared that all the world's sand was sliding into it.

Then the hole began to swell. First with sand and stones, then with the fabric of the settlement itself. Signposts, potted plants, buildings—all were dragged into the swell, which inflated like a frog's throat. Soon, it became clear that there was something within the swell: a head. A giant's head, larger than a house, made from the materials of the desert itself. A body followed, and in seconds the settlement that had been around the trees was turned into dust and subsumed into the giant's growing body.

The people fleeing the swell looked like ants to Ethike. Most of the people were on foot—small black dots scrambling in a disoriented panic—but there were riders on camelback as well, speeding outward in every direction. Even a camel's gallop wasn't enough, however, and soon camels and riders were tossed into the air as the desert beneath them was yanked into the swell.

One of those dots, Ethike knew, was Zogo. One the red-silked man.

One was Silah.

Two people on foot outran even the camels. Aza and Silah's guardsman. The soldiers. They were armored in scales of iridescent light, sprinting at impossible speeds away from the gravity of the swell. They kept their pace long enough that they were still alive when the swelling stopped.

The result was a giant made of sand. Of the desert itself. A vaguely human-shaped roiling mass of sand and brick, plants and people, anything unfortunate enough to be sucked into its bulk. Even beside the impossibly large trees, the giant was an overwhelming sight.

This was the Ajungo, Ethike realized. The monster of legend. The rage of the Forever Desert itself. Somehow, something had caused it to be summoned, and now it was unleashed again on mortals. But the stories were wrong. No amount of sacrifice could placate this beast, whether ears, eyes, or tongue. It had emerged to exact a price that only it could comprehend, and they were all there to suffer for it.

Then the glowing soldiers sped into sight. Fists reared back, encased in the light of the Seer, Aza and her comrade soared high into the air, speeding toward the giant, propelled by a swirl of sand that had launched them from the earth. They had decided to fight the desert itself, and though he feared for their safety, Ethike knew better than to doubt them. He'd seen what they did to the bagoba. This giant had no eyes or ears or any way, that Ethike could tell, of understanding that it was about to be dealt a blow from two soldiers of the Seeing Arts.

Despite that, the giant raised an arm and brought it down, swiping

Aza and her fellow Seer in midair and effortlessly smearing them into the sand, their bones turned into white paste among a splotch of red.

The impact sent a wall of sand rippling in all directions. Ethike turned his mount and sped away from the approaching wave, but he knew he would be too slow. The sand was over a dozen feet high and traveling twice as fast as any camel could. It soon caught him, ripping him off his mount, sending him flipping over himself in an impenetrable storm.

His final thought, before the world-blackening crash of his body against the earth, was that there was something very fair about what had happened. How much blood had been spilled when those people's hands were severed? How many horrors had been carried out in naked view of the sun and sand? All those years and no one had devised a better way of life than unabashed cruelty.

And the Forever Desert had witnessed everything. Until it had finally decided to release the might of the Ajungo and put an end to it.

10

THE FIRST THING ETHIKE noticed was that he was still alive. As the sand had overtaken him, he had been so confident of his impending death that he hadn't even bothered to pray—he'd assumed he was moments away from meeting the Goddess Herself.

The second thing he noticed was that he wasn't buried beneath a dozen feet of sand. Instead, he was on his back, staring up into a dark sky.

Lastly, he noticed that he wasn't alone.

He wasn't quite sure how he knew that—he had watched every single soul in the City of Truth perish. Still, he could feel another presence.

His body screamed in protest as he sat up, but, blessedly, nothing was broken. He looked around and saw no one. He stood and looked around again, and only then did he see the body splayed out on the desert floor, brushed in sand as if it had been there so long the desert had begun burying it. As he approached, he noticed how small the body was.

A boy.

He was in fine black silks, as fine as any travel-wear Ethike had seen, with sturdy leather boots. His face was young, scarcely approaching teenage years, and was stuck in a pained frown, as if in the throes of a nightmare. Ethike would have assumed him to be from the City of a Thousand Stories if it weren't for the infantile, fully formed ears on either side of his head.

Like Silah.

It occurred to him again that Silah was dead. Zogo, Aza, Silah's companions. All killed by the Ajungo. And he, their oft opposed leader, had escaped without injury. He couldn't help imagining their final moments, gazing up at a malevolent mountain of desert, more confused than desperate. And then their bodies began to rip apart. What hope could there be in such an ending? Ethike thought to leave the boy, allow him to mercifully transition from a temporary sleep to an eternal one. Better that than the prolonged, dehydrated death that likely awaited Ethike.

But the boy's eyes fluttered open, and the thought was erased from Ethike's mind.

"Are you okay?" he signed.

The boy scrambled to a seated position. Fear rang him like a bell, primal and trembling.

"It is fine," Ethike signed. "You are safe." He put his palms face out, slowly so as to calm the boy. "What is your name?" He gradually offered his hand to help the boy up.

The boy watched Ethike's hands like they were twin serpents with ten tongues. Ethike maintained his posture patiently, neither advancing nor withdrawing. He let the boy navigate his fear—wrestle with it—and was heartened when the boy stilled and took his hand.

Ethike pulled him to his feet.

"My name is Ethike," he signed.

The boy waited a while before responding. "Nice . . . to . . . meet you."

He signed like he had only just learned to use his fingers. Each sign was slightly distorted, enough that Ethike had to watch closely to be sure he understood them.

"Do you have a name?" Ethike signed.

The boy didn't answer, and Ethike saw that the boy was not capable of answering any more questions. Judging from his fine clothes, he was the son of some ogisi from the City of Truth. He'd just seen the annihilation of his home, the disintegration of his parents, the scattering of everything he'd ever known. It is a cruel thing when people are forced to rebuild a life that has only just begun.

"Even deserts have a beginning," Ethike signed. He'd never been good about finding consoling words. His vocabulary was too functional, not emotive enough. When he reached for words in times of distress, all he found were the ones that had been trained into him.

"This is the first Memento of the Ogisi," he continued, "passed down over the centuries. It means . . ." He thought of how he could explain it to the boy in a way that would bolster his spirits. "It means that everything has to start somewhere. And this is where you start. Don't worry about anything before this. I know that may be difficult to imagine, but . . ."

The boy didn't say anything back, but he did stare long at Ethike, and in his eyes was a dark and terrible weight, as if he were making a decision that would determine the fate of the world.

Then it passed, and the boy seemed to warm the slightest bit before turning away.

He was so small. So fragile. The Forever Desert had just crushed Ethike's friends, a wound so fresh that there hadn't yet been time to feel it. The Ajungo was nowhere in sight—perhaps it had been sated. Perhaps not.

Either way, at that moment, Ethike made a vow. It was the same vow he'd made six years prior, after pulling Uwi's crying, blood-streaked form from the wreckage of their collapsed family home. He would care for this boy. He would teach the boy. Whatever challenges the boy faced in the years ahead, whatever cruel terrors life visited upon him, Ethike would guide him through them. Ethike would never know how or why the boy had survived the settlement's destruction, but he knew it was only by divine providence—the protection of the Goddess Herself.

He sealed the vow with a prayer to the Goddess, that She make him into the kind of man who could give the boy the life he deserved.

And the Goddess answered his prayer.

To Ethike's misfortune.

*   *   *

As they traveled the desert, Ethike could think of nothing to say to the boy but to tell him about the world outside the City of Truth. Maybe because he was an ogisi and long-winded explanations came instinctively to him. Maybe it was a way of feeling like he was with Uwi, walking back home from a day at the Great Temple of Osi, drinking in the nighttime glow of the City of a Thousand Stories.

Whatever the motivation, he enjoyed painting the boy a picture of the broader world. He told him about the city, a place as full of trees as the desert was with sand. He described for him the sight of the black spires of the Great Temples against a bright blue sky, the way the three rivers seasoned the skin with moisture, the crunch, then cottony softness of a fresh loaf from the Ihenwele bakery. He told him some of the histories, about Obasa and Illami and a few others.

The boy never replied. Other than his initial words upon waking, he didn't sign at all. But he watched thirstily, as absorbed in the stories as Uwi always was. Likely, Ethike's stories were the first the boy had ever heard about a place that wasn't dusted in sand and where people weren't forced to wear their severed hands around their throats. Ethike liked to believe his stories brought the boy hope, helped him cope with the punishing sun, rationed food and water, and arduous trekking.

One afternoon, when they'd settled down to rest, Ethike told a story about Uwi.

"She lost her family," he signed, "as you did. And she is curious, as you are. She is ten—that must be about your age?"

The boy didn't respond.

"In any case, she is the best thing in my life. I hope the two of you may be friends."

Ethike kept watch as the boy slept, and he did his best to keep them out of the sun and heat. Despite how few supplies they had, they made consistent progress, and the boy seemed to grow more comfortable with both Ethike and the world, sweating out his pain and drinking down the waters of a new life. Once, when their rations were depleted, the boy reached into the chest of his silk robes and produced two smooth red apples, as fresh as if just plucked from the tree. He leaned forward and pressed one into Ethike's hand, then scooted a safe distance away to enjoy his own.

Ethike suspected he would never fully know what the boy had been through, but the gesture showed there was love in him, and kindness, and it was those qualities that Ethike decided to define the boy by.

They eventually made it back to the wagon, where the massive bones of the bagoba's body had been picked clean by scavengers. They drank their fill of water from the still-surging spring and recovered important supplies. They spent a whole day there recuperating their energy, and the boy seemed to enjoy the break. His usual stoicism briefly yielded to relief as he lay down on the carpeted wagon floor, rubbing the ache from his feet.

But then it was time to go, and Ethike saw the unmistakable clench of fear tighten across the boy's face as he looked out across the expanse of desert that still lay ahead of them.

"Even gardens have an end," he signed.

The boy's eyes slid sharply toward Ethike.

"The second Memento of the Ogisi," he continued. "It means . . .

that everything has to end at some point. So let it end and be grateful for what it was. Again, this may be difficult, but . . ."

For a moment, the boy wore the same face as before, the one laden with decision, eyes soft with uncertainty. Then he picked up his new travel satchel—one of Zogo's that had been left behind—and climbed down from the wagon.

As they grew closer to the city, Ethike did his best to prepare the boy for city life, explaining to him how small their home would be, how school would work, and more. He also described all the delicious foods he would enjoy and the animals he could pet. He'd hoped for some reaction from the boy, but he never got much more than that weighing stare.

Soon, the city's walls appeared on the horizon, a stark black boundary holding back the gold flood of the Forever Desert. A well of tears sprung so suddenly and forcefully from Ethike that the boy backed away, and Ethike was too overcome to reassure him. He yearned again for the scent of wood and for stacks of books around him. He craved a day devoted to nothing but research and holding Uwi, to lifting and twirling her around in the air like she deserved.

Moreover, the sight of the city reminded him that he was returning without any of his companions. Zogo and Aza. And Silah. He missed them very much. They had not been his friends for long, but friendship is measured in depth, not length, and their shared days of doubt and dehydration had bonded them.

"Halt!" a guard signed from atop a guard tower as Ethike and the boy approached. "Name yourselves."

Ethike raised his hands to answer, but he felt a weight settle into one of them, holding it in place. When he looked down, he found the boy's hand in his own. There was still fear in him, Ethike saw. More fear than any boy ought to live with. But as often as fear could erode trust, it could also drive someone toward it, the drowning ant clinging to the drifting branch.

Trust is the only coin that doubles when spent.

"I am Ogisi Ethike," he signed with his free hand. "And I have returned with the treasure from Osi's Tomb."

11

HE WAS TAKEN STRAIGHT to the Capitol, where he was fed and bathed and given a fresh black igbulu, befitting his status as an ogisi. He insisted that the boy not be separated from him at any point, and the guards respected the request, eyeing him and the boy with curiosity.

When he was called before the Elders, though, he had to go alone.

"I will return," he signed.

Yet the boy wouldn't let him go. He signed no words, made no expressions. But in his eyes was a desperation that rooted Ethike's feet. It was the first time they would be apart since their meeting in the desert, and it was clear the boy had no desire to revisit the uncertainty and isolation he felt when he had woken up with Ethike's face above him.

Ethike crouched down and laid a gentle hand on the boy's shoulder.

"You remember my niece?" he signed. "Uwi. The one I have told you about?"

He nodded.

"When I return, we will go join Uwi. And you will have someone to play with. What do you think of that?"

The boy thoroughly searched Ethike's eyes. What he was searching for, Ethike did not know. But he held eye contact and opened up his heart to the boy, and he trusted that truth and love and kindness were a universal language.

"My name," the boy signed, "is Agba."

Ethike wrapped him in a smothering embrace. Agba stiffened before melting into him, yielding, for a moment, some of the weight he carried through the world. Ethike accepted the burden for what it was—a gift. There is no finer gift an adult can receive than a child unburdening their strife.

"Even water has a story," Ethike signed. "The third and final Memento of the Ogisi. It means . . . it means that there is always something between the beginning and the end. And that is where life happens. We will live this life together, Agba."

Ethike took a deep breath and flashed a final smile, then was gone.

In the throne room, the Elders sat their high-backed wooden thrones in front of the waterfall that fell endlessly from the ceiling into the floor. Ethike savored the moistness of the air against his skin. It was like his pores were breathing, his exhales and inhales trading the dry dust within him for a refreshing coolness.

He prostrated himself, crossing his arms over his chest and touching his head to the floor before rising up to his knees.

"Honored Elders," he signed. "I come to you in humility, with my report from Osi's Tomb."

He had no doubt they'd been informed beforehand of what he was there to do, but his words were nonetheless met with stillness, bronze masks betraying nothing.

"Did you find it?" they asked, their fingers flashing in unison.

"Honored Elders, I did. And with it, I found the truth."

They shared glances and shifted in their seats before responding. "Go on."

He told them everything. From the moment he left the city walls to his discovery of the Aleke and the City of Truth to his return. Little of it pertained directly to Osi's Tomb, but he understood his testimony was a historical one, and this was his last chance to enshrine his memories of his friends.

He concluded with the part of the story that had been gnawing at him most.

"Honored Elders, there were people in the settlement," he began, "who were not treated as people. They do not communicate as we do—they use their mouths rather than their hands. But they are humans still, and are deserving of equal dignity. I believe the stories of the Ajungo's song comes from how these people speak. But they are not the Ajungo. They are not monsters, and they cannot hurt us. I know the Silence is our tradition, but I am now convinced it is not needed. We do not need protection from these people. The people, in truth, need protection from us. From the ogisi."

The Elders nodded, clearly listening closely.

"You said the sand giant destroyed everything," they asked. "Are you certain?"

Ethike nodded. "Sadly."

"And this boy you returned with? Where is he from?"

He hadn't mentioned Agba. Partially because he was not relevant, and partially to further protect the boy's already fragile sense of privacy.

"Honored Elders, I confess I do not know," he signed. "But I believe him to be from the destroyed settlement. I suspect he is a child of an ogisi."

The Elders didn't respond to that. They didn't refute him, but they also gave him no sign that they accepted his words.

"Ogisi Ethike," they signed after a pause, their hands flicking forcefully. "You will speak not of your time outside the city. You will make no written records and will hand over any existing records for disposal. As well, you will hand the boy over to us. In exchange—"

"Honored Elders"—he shook his head—"with respect, this seems ill-considered." He regretted his phrasing as soon as he signed it. "This knowledge—"

"—we will continue to care for Uwi and will triple the size of the Great Temple of Osi."

Perhaps, before his journey, something like that would have meant something to him. He'd always wanted to give Uwi the life she deserved. But he'd seen too much death in the desert. Life was too fickle, too hard, to be summed up by good schools and comfortable beds.

"Honored Elders," he signed with apology, "I believe this truth must be shared. If for nothing else than to cease the practice of the Silence. The city needs—"

"Understood, Ogisi Ethike," they signed with finality.

There was a long stretch during which nothing was gestured. The Elders simply looked between one another, nodding. Then, finally:

"You are correct," they signed. "We will reveal your findings to the people. You will allow us a week to prepare, after which we will call upon you."

Ethike exhaled an appreciative breath and prostrated himself again. "Honored Elders, thank you. Your wisdom abounds."

When leaving the Aleke's palace, Ethike had questioned devoting his life to the pursuit of truth. Yet as he left the Elders' throne room, he had never felt more certain of the course of his life. The people of the city would learn of the crimes being perpetrated in their name.

They would learn that there were other people in the Forever Desert, like them in some ways and different in others. Most importantly, they would learn that the Ajungo they feared was not what they thought, that their children no longer needed to be maimed, and that the quest for the legendary tomb was best forgotten.

Ethike turned his mind to the joys of the future. Seeing Uwi and Agba meet for the first time. Building a home for the three of them. Taking his life in a new direction altogether, one that would see him focused more on the present than the past, more concerned with stories of the people in the city than those of the Forever Desert.

Each step across the tiled Capitol floors toward his chambers brought him closer to his new life, further from his old. It was time, he realized, to write his own story.

Even deserts have a beginning.

Even gardens have an end.

Even water has a story.

But when he returned to his chambers, Agba was gone.

PART II
AGBA

12

AGBA ALWAYS KNEW HE was destined for greatness.

He was the Ogisi. The Last Child of Tutu. Inheritor of the Wisdom of the Garden. None of that meant anything to Agba, but it meant something to everyone else. Every morning, the other Children of Tutu started their days by passing by him with their heads bowed.

"Blessed morning, Ogisi," they whispered with reverence.

"Blessings upon you, Ogisi," they called with adoration.

"Papa Tutu shield you, Ogisi," they proclaimed with passion.

Often, they would give him a gift or a hug or a warm smile. Then they would leave the shelter of the Garden—the fertile, emerald space at the center of the Great Trees—and go off to work in the city.

Only his baba was different. Instead of passing by with a prayer, Baba would stop just inside the mighty trunks of the Great Trees and extend his sturdy branch arms. Agba would rush into them, then be whisked up into the air for an embrace. That brief moment of ascent, faster and higher than his best jump could take him, was the best feeling in Agba's world. For that moment, the birds were his peers, the giant trees merely his perches. He was the king of the sky, soaring above his subjects.

"Learn well, my son," Baba would say, his voice a boulder that could not be moved. "Only by learning can you free us."

Approaching his teenage years, Agba found himself hating most things. But Baba's embraces were evergreen, the rare thing that felt as good yesteryear as it would in the years to come. When he was set back to the ground, Agba would watch his baba climb over bulging roots and between giant trunks as he followed the other adults to the outside world.

As Agba grew and learned to climb, he tried to recreate the soaring feeling of his baba's embraces by scaling the branches of the smaller trees. It was slow, and difficult, but each year he got faster and rose higher, and soon he could watch from above as Baba emerged from the Garden and continued into the desert, melding seamlessly into the crisscrossing humanity.

"Ogisi Agba!"

Greatmama's voice only came in two volumes: shriek and whisper. This one was a shriek.

"Ogisi Agba! Come and sit for your lesson!"

Despite being the Ogisi, Agba still had to spend hours each day at the feet of his greatmama. There, she would tell him stories about people and places and times long past. Sometimes, he listened. Sometimes, he stared up at the sky, that tiny disc of blue that was the only thing higher than the Garden's Great Trees, and wondered if there was an end to learning. One day, he imagined, he would be an adult and then he would just live how he wanted and eat what he liked and fulfill his duty as the Ogisi, whatever it was.

That day, the stories were some of his favorites. The story of how Greatmama met Greatbaba. The story of Agba's birth and his mama's death—how Mama had made a deal with Papa Tutu to exchange her life for Agba's. The story of the long drought from Greatmama's childhood, when people had turned to drinking blood to survive.

The final story of the day was one he'd heard hundreds of times before—the story of the Aleke.

"He came from a land called the City of Lies," Greatmama began, "led by people called the Ajungo. He arrived one day with his merchants and soldiers and physicians. When your greatbaba and I went out to meet him, we were surprised to find we shared a common language, and many common interests. We even shared a meal. For many months, there was a friendship. We would leave the Garden to visit with the Aleke and his disciples from the City of Lies. Then one day, they asked to enter the Garden."

Agba didn't know how old his greatmama was, but he knew that her body was full of pain and her mind was full of memories. So when she looked up at the trees in the middle of the story, he just assumed it was something that came with being old, like she was taking a break from remembering.

"As you know," she continued, "the Garden is only for the Children of Tutu. So we refused. And when the Aleke ordered us killed, his own merchants opposed it, for they enjoyed trading with us for the sweet fruits of our Garden. But the Aleke is clever."

The Aleke began to spread a rumor that the merchants were trai-tors, Greatmama explained. A simple lie that grew until anyone seen speaking with the Children of Tutu became so detestable that they would do anything to prove their loyalty.

"Speak with those savages!?" the merchants cried. "Better to lose our tongues!"

The Aleke's merchants cut off their tongues so that they could never again be accused of speaking with the enemy.

That was when the war began. The Aleke's soldiers had iron weapons and ghostly skin that could withstand any blow and return it tenfold. Most of the Children stayed within the protection of the Garden, but those who went out were slain. In little time, the bodies of Children sat in wet red piles, and their anguished pleas and rattling final breaths became so loud that many of the Aleke's soldiers sought an end to the violence. So the Aleke spread a lie that these soldiers were traitors, and soon the accused again had to prove their loyalty.

"Listen to those savages!?" the soldiers cried. "Better to lose our ears!"

The Aleke's soldiers cut off their ears so that they could never again be accused of listening to the enemy.

Once all those Children who left the safety of the Garden to fight were murdered to the last, the Aleke had his soldiers light fires all around the Great Trees and fan the smoke into the Garden.

"For seventy-seven days and nights we suffered," Greatmama said, her eyes glazed over with a film of moisture. "I watched our elders and children choke and die. In the end, we had no choice."

All the Children of Tutu left the protection of the Garden to face the Aleke. First, they tried to negotiate, but the merchants couldn't speak to them in return. Then they begged, but the soldiers couldn't hear them. So they got down on their knees and raised their hands in complete surrender so that all could understand, hoping the Aleke still had humanity enough in him to relent.

"But he had no humanity," Greatmama said, "so when he saw shame and sympathy in the eyes of his disciples, he could not allow it. For the Aleke is cruel."

The Aleke ordered the removal of the Children's hands. This time, the physicians spoke up in protest, claiming that watching innocents suffer harm would violate their oaths. By then, the Aleke was well practiced in accusing his own people of treachery.

"Watch those savages!?" the physicians cried. "Better to lose our eyes!"

"So he took our hands," Greatmama said, raising her stumps, "and tied them around our necks so that we may forever remember the consequence of resistance."

That was where Greatmama stopped and looked over Agba's shoulder. But when Agba looked back, he saw nothing. Just the dense coils of green that made up the Garden floor and the small, round pond at its center.

"And then what?" Agba asked.

Greatmama responded by leaning forward in her chair and poking the tip of his nose. She had been doing it since he was a child. She said his mama had done the same when she was alive. Agba knew he was supposed to be too old for such things, but it still made him giggle no matter how hard he tried not to. "A story to continue on another day, Ogisi Agba," she said.

In all the years of Greatmama's lessons, the story of the Aleke was always left unfinished. And Agba was always left with so many questions—about the Aleke and the history of the Children of Tutu and so much else. There were two questions he'd been asking longest, questions none of Greatmama's stories ever answered.

Why he was the Ogisi? And what did it mean that he was?

13

ONE DAY, AGBA CLIMBED higher than ever before, so high that he had to grab tightly to the tree's trunk, lest the winds yank him off. He looked down at the city around the Garden, almost two dozen buildings scattered in every direction and connected by paths worn in the sand. The Aleke's palace stood out not just for being larger than the other buildings but for the rooftop terrace, where the Aleke spent most of his days.

This time, it wasn't just the Aleke. There were others, visitors judging by their unusual style of dress. Sometimes, he'd forget that there was another city out there with thousands, maybe millions, of people. All serving under the rule of the Ajungo. Like the Aleke and his friends, their fingers contorted in their silent language. With how much he'd watched them over the years, Agba had come to understand some of their speech, and he was continually surprised by how boring their conversations were.

Among the Aleke and his disciples were a dozen Children of Tutu. Even from a great distance, Agba recognized his baba's strong form and straight back. He strode here and there, walking up beside the other Children and giving them directions that they immediately followed. He was the chief servant, and though he did not enjoy his life of servitude, he performed it with the same pride and diligence he did everything else.

Then, one of the Children—Uncle Ojiegbe, who was the Garden's shoemaker—stumbled just enough for the glass of wine between his stumps to slip and shatter, splashing across the rooftop floor.

Agba recoiled, fearful that poor Uncle Ojiegbe would be beaten for the accident. Instead, the Aleke grabbed a serving platter and flung it at the man.

But the platter sailed past Uncle Ojiegbe, curving up and away and embedding itself in another man's skull.

His baba's skull.

After that, Agba couldn't remember much. He couldn't remember how he got back to the ground. He couldn't even remember seeing Baba sprawled on the rooftop, the once-lively man diminishing into death.

All he could remember was the Aleke. The Aleke leaned back in his chair, and the spirit of violence and rage that had filled him moments before suddenly sat dormant in his crossed legs and smiling cheeks. Even hours later, as Greatmama consoled Agba through the delirium of grief, the image of the Aleke was all he could recall.

His greatmama saw that a seed had been planted within her greatson. In her wisdom, she watered it, even as she knew that she might not live to watch it bear fruit. She reached a hand out to Agba, wiping his tears away with the rough skin of her stump.

"Tears are precious, my Agba," she said. "Save them, that you may give them to your enemies."

                    *   *   *

On seven different occasions, Agba tried to escape the Garden. Once, he'd been armed with a knife he stole from his greatmama; twice, he had been armed with sharpened sticks; the other times he'd been armed only with teeth and tears, trusting in the sharp edge of his grief. Each time, the other Children of Tutu restrained him, cradling him in their arms and sharing his tears, making him all manner of promises in attempts to calm him.

"Your baba is with Papa Tutu, Ogisi."

"In time you will heal, Ogisi."

"The Aleke will suffer for this, Ogisi."

But their promises were a mirage that disappeared upon scrutiny. He didn't want promises anyhow. He didn't even want vengeance. Not really.

What he wanted was the most impossible and childish of things: He wanted his baba. He wanted his mama, though he could not remember her. He wanted to sit in his home—a modest but loving thing, carved into the sheltering base of a Great Tree—and enjoy a meal with his family. He wanted the other Children, all his uncles and aunties, to visit with treats and games, to tease him and dance with him and talk late into the night with the other grown-ups, their voices soothing him as he fell asleep. He wanted to take all their hands from around their throats and put them where they were meant to be, where they could nurture the world around them.

He wanted to be happy. He wanted to be free. He wanted the Aleke and the entire City of Lies to be erased from the world.

Days later, in the early hours of the morning, Baba's body was returned. A half dozen Children bore it on their shoulders, covered in a red cloth that might have once been white. Agba refused to look. His last memory of his baba was of a strong man with a perfect smile that dimpled at his cheeks. A man whose embraces were the closest thing to soaring. He had to protect that memory. Against the Aleke and the City of Lies. Even against the truth, if necessary.

Only Greatmama looked upon it. When she did, she immediately collapsed. Not like a felled tree—her whole form crashing and breaking as a single entity—but like a decaying one, each piece of her melting into the unrecognizable before sloughing away. It was too slow a collapse to damage even her old bones but no less violent. Agba rushed over to her to find her stare empty and distant, like when she was lost in times long past.

"Come, my Ogisi Agba," she eventually said. "Come and sit for your final lesson."

She led him to the pond at the center of the Garden and sat him down right along its edge. He'd never been so near it before. The pond was too sacred to drink from—too sacred to touch, even. He was so close that he was able to look into the water's black depths for the first time in his life. His own rippling face looked up from beneath its surface. He had always been told he looked like his mama, but he didn't know her face, so he couldn't say. All he knew was that he looked nothing like his baba. Baba's face was long and angled and strong. But the reflection looking up at him was round and boyish, with ears that stuck out like wings.

Greatmama was looking into the pond as she spoke. "Do you want to know what makes you special, Ogisi Agba?"

All his life, he'd listened to stories of special people. Many of them had suffered and watched loved ones suffer in turn. It was that very suffering that built people into the heroes they were meant to be, a testament to the transformative power of pain.

Yet Agba had suffered and watched those he loved suffer, and he was untransformed. There was only the pain.

So he knew the answer to her question. "Nothing," he said.

"If only that were true," Greatmama said. She sighed and put an arm around his shoulders, pulling him close against her side. "There once was a boy much like you. Born among these very trees, from the waters of this very pond. A boy named Tutu."

Agba had heard the story before. After creating the Garden, Papa Tutu had turned into a human, just like any of them. It was his birth from the pond that had consecrated it, made it untouchable—even a single finger in the pond would fill you with too much power for any mortal thing to hold.

"Within the boy Tutu was a power unlike any other," she continued. "He could see things no human could see, leap higher than the Garden's tallest tree, split the earth with just a stamp of his foot. And once the Ajungo heard about this power, they conspired to steal it for themselves. They killed him with weapons made from iron, his one weakness. Then, in hopes of stealing his power, the Ajungo ate his body and drank his blood.

"But they only gained a trickle. Just enough to make them thirsty for more. This is why they persecute us, Ogisi Agba. They desire more of the power that resides here."

None of this was new to Agba, but he listened anyway. Before, he would have ignored her. He had thought that Greatmama's stories were of the past, that history was something his ancestors had already resolved.

But now he knew better. Evil didn't change. The evil of yesteryear was no different from the evil of today, and the Aleke had shown him that. Agba felt shame that it had taken his baba's death for him to learn the lesson Greatmama had been trying to teach him all along: History was a story with no ending.

"This is why we are the Children of Tutu," Greatmama concluded, and as she said it, the other Children emerged into view. They were all older than Agba, all taller, all of them broken with grief. In their faces, he saw a violent pain that told him how much they loved his baba. And when he realized that his own face must have looked the same, he failed to heed Greatmama's advice of saving his tears for his enemies.

"We are Papa Tutu's legacy," Greatmama said. "And his power has waited here, for the day it would be summoned to end the cruelties of history, to deliver the verdict against our enemies now and forever. That is what 'ogisi' means: one who decides the truth.

"That is why you are special, Ogisi Agba."

His greatmama stood, and suddenly she had never looked older. Her legs were frail, her back crescented, her eyes pouched and heavy. She called a few of the Children forward, Agba's aunties and uncles, and they draped him in the finest black silks Agba had ever seen. They placed on his feet sturdy sandals, far thicker and more comfortable than he'd ever worn. Lastly, Greatmama herself produced a small, leaf-woven pouch that held a few apples inside. She pulled out the neck of his shirt and dropped the pouch of apples in, where it slid down to his waist.

Then Uncle Ojiegbe's voice filled the assembly, the trees, the water, Agba's body. He'd been there at Baba's death, had been the intended target of the Aleke's mad wrath, and his voice was gravel crushed into dust by heartache, a rasp near choking. When he sang, all the Children's voices rose in a cresting harmony, echoing his call.

> Oyeee Ogisi! (Oyeee Ogisi!)
> You were the seed that grew
> And for this day, you were prepared
> To bear a deadly fruit

Then Auntie Eweni led the song, her usually sweet voice soured.

> Oyeee Ogisi! (Oyeee Ogisi!)
> Today your flower blooms
> And through the sand, your feet will trek
> May vengeance carry you

Each of them, all thirty Children of Tutu, sang a verse. Each voice washed over Agba, straightening him only to break him, filling him only to empty him. A dozen times he managed to stop crying and a dozen times he resumed, until, when Greatmama sang the last verse, he could no longer tell whether he was crying or not. Whether he was Agba or whether he was the song itself, a stitching together of all his people's emptied hearts.

Oyeee Ogisi (Oyeee Ogisi!)
Their day is finally due
No suckling's hair shall go unbloodied
Let them remember you

All his life, Agba had questioned what it meant that he was the Ogisi. But by the end of the song, when the voices of the Children of Tutu melded together in the final line, he had no more questions.

Remember Ogisi!
Remember Ogisi!
Remember Ogisi!

In the ensuing silence, with even the birds and branches hushed, Greatmama leaned forward and kissed him on his forehead, her lips so dry they scratched his skin.

"My greatson," she said in a quivering voice. He had never seen Greatmama cry before. Tears dripped from her chin. "May Papa Tutu grant you peace," she prayed. "May Papa Tutu grant you bravery. And when the time comes that you join us in His embrace, may you be remembered truly."

Then she shoved her stumps into him, and Agba fell back. The image of his weeping Greatmama receded until his back burst against the surface of the pond.

14

EVERYTHING WAS DIFFERENT under the surface. There was a delay when he moved, action disconnected from thought, water folding around him. He moved himself, arms pushing water aside as if he were wading through tree branches. Yet he continued to sink, and silent bubbles escaped his lips. The light of the surface soon dimmed to black.

He drifted for a while. He swam. He tried to go up, but in the pitch blackness, he didn't know where up was. Then he bumped against something firm. He reached into the darkness and touched what felt like a pile of rocks. Dozens of spheres, hard and round beneath his fingers.

Then he felt a sucking wind, the water drawing him into the pebbles, then ever so slightly pushing him away. In then out. In then out again. Inhale then exhale. Breathing.

He realized at that moment that he was in the presence of something very large. And very alive.

In surprise, from his inexperience with water, Agba gasped. The water filled the vacuum of his body without hesitation, through throat and nose and the slips of space around his eyes. He was the water, and the water was him, and his limbs were currents, and his mind was its bottomless depth.

Blackness.

Nothing.

Everything.

Stars gleamed like scattered sand on a moonlit night. All around him were more of the same, an endless field of densely packed stars. Among them were spheres like tiny berries, each their own size and pattern of melding hues. One of the spheres, he somehow knew, was the world. The whole of it, not just the Garden or the desert, but all the lands beyond too, bound up in a tiny ball no larger than his fist, spinning in the distance among the others.

Then there was movement. A tiny point of light drifting toward him, closer and closer until he could see legs in its brightness, and a head, and a long torso that ended in a longer tail.

It was a lizard. A great lizard glimmering with a powerful iridescence, as large as the world itself—each scale a star, each eye a city, each claw a mountain. Wings the size of continents were tucked against Her sides. Where She passed, She authored beauty into existence, and in Her wake were symphonies of color, conversing in shifting shapes among swirls of stars. There was a peace that emanated from Her, and as Her enormity passed by him, She introduced herself, granting Agba the Gift of knowledge.

She was known in many ways.

The Queen of the Heavens.

The source of all truth.

The Goddess.

But Her oldest and truest name: The Ogisi.

She had drifted like this since before the first thought was thought, birthing worlds with a bend of Her wings, sculpting life with each blink of Her eyes. As She passed through the black ink of the heavens, those creatures with the wherewithal to perceive Her were able to draw on Her power, allowing them to join Her as authors of beauty.

Then Agba was in a world of endless forest. Trees that were leagues high provided shade for seas of glistening fruit, an infinity of giant beasts, rivers as wide as they were long. There was no sand in sight. Not a single grain. This world teemed with life, all of it enlarged and engorged a thousandfold.

And within the enormity of life, there were people. Entire tribes living within the cavernous hollows of the tallest trees, and Agba suddenly stood among them. They were naked and small; even the adults were no bigger than he. Their faces were wide and blunt, their eyes dull and fearful. In the back of one hollow, babies clung to their mamas' chests, while the other adults sat in small groups near the hollow's mouth.

Three adults near the mouth stared up at the purpling sky. There, The Ogisi—at this distance just a point of light—arced from west to east. The adults knelt and raised their hands, eyes closed.

"Oooogiiiisiiii," they chanted. "Oooogiiiisiiii. Oooogiiiisiiii."

As they called upon Her power, pleading for the Gift the creature so freely gave, their skin glittered to life, each pore taking on the faintest spark of light, mirroring the starred skin of the Goddess to whom they prayed. Then the rest of the tribe joined, all of them on their knees, their arms raised. Throughout the forest, the hollows of distant trees began to shine with answered prayers.

First, they fashioned shelter, reshaping the trees to better protect them from the elements. Then, they created fire, around which they huddled long into the night, singing and dancing and praising their new Goddess.

Then, they learned to kill.

They started with the birds of prey, beasts thrice their size whose narrow beaks dipped into tree hollows and feasted on human flesh. Then it was the bears who ate the same fruit the tribes most preferred.

Then, it was each other.

Agba watched war be born, hordes of men and women, strengthened by the power of their Goddess, ripping apart their enemies. They knocked over trees filled with thousands of people, generations crushed by a single crash, entire family lines extinguished.

Eventually, a tribe leader named Shokolokobangoshe chose to pray rather than fight. He and his entire tribe prayed unceasingly, day and night, drinking in as much of The Ogisi's power as they could. When other tribes saw the bright light emanating from Shokolokobangoshe's tree, they paused in their war to pray as well, and soon the whole world was on its knees, beseeching the Goddess's power.

In the sky, The Ogisi's light gradually brightened. At first, Agba assumed it was the power of the prayers, but he soon realized that She was simply drawing closer. She descended from the heavens, growing from a star to a moon, and from a moon to something vaster and more terrifying, an orb enveloped in flame.

They had taken too much, Agba knew. Or perhaps She had given too much. Either way, She lacked the energy even to drift the heavens, and She became an apocalyptic body, crashing into the world that had consumed Her. One second, the humans were swelling fat on the power of their goddess, dreaming of the war they hoped to soon win. The next second, the world was a fractured ball drifting through its own debris cloud within the black void. Everything that had lived upon it was dead—the trees, the animals, the people. Even the rivers were blasted away, leaving a world covered only in the pulverized remains of the pale gold stone that slept deep within the planet.

It was a desert. Empty and endless.

Then all went black again, and Agba found himself still in the pond, filled by its water. Yet he wasn't drowning. He opened his eyes and was surprised to see a faint light shining from his skin, illuminating the area around him in all directions. He could see The Ogisi directly in front of him, curled up within the core of the world that had been built on top of Her body.

She had been there for millennia, dying—for Her, quickly; for humans, infinitely slowly. Her decaying skin was crumbling into round, black balls. Her blood gushed out of Her in clean, clear streams—it was the very water he swam in.

Agba was not the Ogisi he'd believed himself to be—but he was The Ogisi's messenger. His mission was twofold: to save not just his people, but to save Her as well. To do this, She had granted him knowledge of the world that no other living being possessed.

Only by learning can you free us.

There was nothing left for him to learn.

The only thing left to do was free his people.

15

THE WHOLE DESERT DREW into him. Sand crushed away the water, wave after wave of coarse gold slamming into the ignited surface of his skin. As The Ogisi's knowledge expanded his mind, so too did Her power—Her Gift—expand his body. He was boundless. His arms were the smooth sculpt of dunes; his legs were a fused wall of sand; his head a boulder high in the air, ten times higher than he'd ever climbed up the Great Trees.

Below him, Agba watched miniature people scurry from the ruins of the Aleke's palace. The rest of the town was much the same, a graveyard of scattered bricks at the foot of the still-standing Great Trees. He was too high up to distinguish one person from the other. They were all so small. So fragile. Whereas he was the desert, armored in sand, their bodies were mosquito-brittle. Flecks of black crawling across a gold expanse.

He smashed them as easily as blinking. Black flecks turned red. One of those, he was dimly aware, was the Aleke. Hundreds of years of cruelty, extinguished by a child's infinite and vengeful fist. Centuries of terror buried by sand.

Then the Aleke's soldiers attacked. There were two of them in full ghostskin, twin orbs of ascending light. Greatmama had told him so many stories about the Aleke's warriors. They were said to be inhuman, to possess a taste for human flesh, and were nearly indestructible. None of the Children had ever successfully slain one of the soldiers.

For Agba, it took a mere wave of his arm. Their soft innards squished out like squeezed grapes onto his palm. They were close enough to his face that he was able to witness their last moments. One of them, a woman nearly as short as Greatmama, had an expression of such ferocity that gave way—at the last second—to a panicked regret, a moment of pleading and confusion and horror that lasted only as long as it took for her to inhale a scream she would never release.

Then she was gone, a lumpy red rain drizzling onto the sand.

Then there was pain.

Agba felt a thousand hot spears ramming through him. He felt his rib cage dissolve, his brains burst, his limbs stretch themselves in every direction before exploding off him, as if yanked by galloping camels. Pain so maddening it sent his mind screaming for his great-mama's soothing voice, for Baba's strong hands to lift him higher, out of his body of sand, into the safety of his embrace.

But neither Greatmama nor Baba came. Instead, the sand fell away, and he was just a boy again, plummeting headfirst from the sky and crashing into the sand, removing both the pain and his consciousness.

* * *

To create is divine; to destroy, human.

All who sought The Ogisi were given freely of Her power, for that was Her way. When mortals used Her power to destroy, however—a corruption of its purpose—there was a price. Whatsoever destruction the wielder inflicted on others, they themselves would feel. Yet even that divine deterrent could not stay humanity's bloodlust, and thus the earliest people discovered that The Ogisi's price could be eluded by paying another—the price of their humanity. They numbed themselves so that they felt no more pain when tearing out the throats of their enemies than they did rubbing two sticks together to make fire.

Agba had felt nothing as he crushed the Aleke and dozens of others. They were just flecks. Grains of sand. It was killing the soldiers that had hurt him. Even in their ghostskin, they looked like people to him. That brief moment before he ended their lives had been enough to make numbing himself impossible.

He was disappointed in himself. And afraid. He was disappointed that he had failed to numb himself. But that was a problem easily fixed in time. The fear was of a deeper nature, and the immediate pain in his heart told him it was a true fear.

What if he didn't want to kill?

Greatmama. The Children. The Ogisi. All of them were depending on him ridding the world of the Ajungo. What if he was the wrong choice? He was just a boy with no training. He liked to joke tough, but he'd never been able to hurt anything, not really.

Remember Ogisi.

He had to remember. Greatmama's stories, The Ogisi's vision. Baba.

He had to remember.

Too gradually, the pain passed. When he felt strong enough, he used the Gift again. All his senses were enhanced and intermingled; everything the desert could feel, so could he. The dead bodies buried in the sand weighed on his skin. The ruins of the Aleke's palace sounded like teeth bouncing off each other. The wheeling grunts of the approaching vultures were the taste of bile.

He released the Gift just in time to see a figure standing over him, shadowed by the sun. Its fingers contorted into a series of shapes. *Are you okay?*

Agba drew back, scrambling to a seated position. The shadow resolved into the image of a large man, though he held a cautious posture that made him seem smaller than he was.

It is fine, Fingers said. *You are safe.* Yet he put his palms face out, and Agba could only imagine he was preparing to shoot fire from his palms or some other such evil magic. Instead, his fingers twisted and twirled again. *What is your name?*

Fingers extended a hand down.

A hand. Agba's wits finally and fully returned to him.

Fingers was from the City of Lies.

Agba should have killed him. That was his mission. That was the only way to free the Children, to avenge The Ogisi. He wouldn't even need the full power of his Gift. A sand-armored fist could rip through the man, pull his insides out. Agba tried to think of Fingers not as a human but as Ajungo, as an accomplice in Baba's death.

But this wasn't the Aleke. The Aleke was dead. Fingers was just a man wandering the desert, offering Agba help to his feet. He likely thought Agba to be another survivor of the town's destruction. No matter how deeply Agba searched within himself, he could find no numbness. The thought of killing another person unnumbed brought vomit quivering up his throat. He swallowed it down.

Then he reached up and took Fingers' hand.

Once Agba was upright, the man's fingers squirmed again.

My name is Ethike.

If Agba spoke with his mouth, this Ethike man would know where he was from. Ethike would try to kill him, and Agba would have to react. He didn't want to kill this man. In fact, he realized this man was his only way of finding where the City of Lies was.

This Ethike could be his guide through the desert.

Agba's mind flashed through all the Ajungo language he knew. *Nice . . . to . . . meet you.*

Do you have a name? Ethike signed.

Agba wasn't certain how to introduce himself in their language, so he just kept quiet. He would have to play a role, he realized. If it was power the Ajungo wanted, then the only path to peace for Agba was powerlessness. To be as helpless and fearful and meek as he could manage.

Ethike looked at him with an expression no one had ever looked at Agba with before. Pity.

Even deserts have a beginning, he said, and Agba froze. *This is the first Memento of The Ogisi.*

It was such a strange thing to say, with no discernible reason for it to have been said. The Ethike man went on to say something about hope or goodness or some such thing—Agba wasn't listening.

Instead, he beheld Ethike with a newfound suspicion, a fear he didn't have to perform. What did this man know, Agba wondered, about the history of the Forever Desert? What did he know about The Ogisi?

Agba could not find it in himself to kill Ethike. But now he saw that the man knew things, and knowledge could be a power more dangerous than any other.

16

THE SUN GLARED DOWN throughout the day, baking air and sand and everything beneath its gaze. In the Garden, there was shade and moisture in abundance. The desert held neither.

As they traveled, Agba tried to maintain a careful distance. He realized that when he destroyed the Ajungo and their City of Lies, he would likely have to kill Ethike too. So he began the process of numbing himself, disguising it as fear. As they trekked through the nights and rested when the sun came up, Agba never spoke, neither with mouth nor hands. It wasn't as difficult as it could have been— Ethike talked enough for the both of them.

My city is a beautiful place, his fingers slithered. *Do you know what a city is?*

He'd heard stories about the City of Lies his entire life, but he didn't really know what a city was. Sometimes he imagined it to be like the Aleke's town, full of tiny buildings and cruel people living in them. Other times, he imagined it to be like the Garden, with great buildings towering into the sky instead of Great Trees, and a bunch of aunties and uncles to play with. But he could never imagine what it smelled like, or which fruit people ate, or if they all sat and listened to stories like he did.

But Agba didn't say anything.

Well, you will see, Ethike added with a smile.

He did that often. Smile. What he had to smile about, Agba didn't know, but each time he did it, Agba felt conflicted. Smiles were lovely things—Agba himself liked smiling, and liked making others smile. But Ethike's smiles made it more difficult for Agba to numb himself. Ethike had a kind smile, a hopeful one, and sometimes as they lay down on the sand to sleep for the day, Agba almost found himself smiling back.

Ethike told a lot of stories as well. He wasn't a bad storyteller, but he wasn't as good as Greatmama—his delivery was stiff and he often

veered down unrelated paths for long stretches. Still, he was enter-
taining enough to help pass the time.

Most of the stories were about the same man—a failed conqueror
named Osi who left the safety of his friends and family to roam the
desert in pursuit of forgettable deeds. It was clear Ethike had such
admiration for Osi that he had patterned his own life after the man.
Yet Osi was believed to have died with no children or land or power.
His life had been fruitless and his death had been unremarkable, and
he'd been promptly forgotten by all but Ethike.

Agba didn't understand it. Papa Tutu was a hero—his story was
full of bravery and courage. Osi's story, as far as Agba could see, was a
miserable one, full of sad errors and meaningless ends.

Papa Tutu's story was an inspiration; Osi's, a cautionary tale.

That is why I came here, Ethike said after another sad Osi story. *I
was seeking Osi's Tomb. The stories imply that upon his death he buried
the truth of my city's history. If I had found it . . .* He shook his head.

When he wasn't talking about Osi, Ethike talked about his niece,
Uwi. Agba had seen Ajungo children his own age before. They enjoyed playing and laughing and eating just as he did. They looked
almost innocent. Sometimes, caught up in Ethike's stories, he'd wonder what Uwi was like, but then he would stop himself so that he
would still be numb to her when he met her. But this only made him
think about Uwi more.

After one long story about Uwi, Ethike fell uncharacteristically
quiet. He remained that way for hours, trudging through the sand,
digging their resting spot at the base of a dune, then lying down for
first watch without another story, or even another word.

Agba pretended to sleep for a long while, then actually fell asleep
for a short while, before waking to find Ethike withdrawn and thick-
eyed. Despite himself, and despite all his attempts to numb himself
to the man, Agba didn't enjoy seeing Ethike sad. He thought about
what he could do to make the man feel better. When Agba got sad,
he liked to climb the Great Trees and eat fruit while the wind blew
louder than his thoughts.

There were no Great Trees in the desert.

But there was fruit.

Agba reached into the chest of his silk robes, into the pouch Greatmama had given him, and produced two of the smooth red apples.

He pressed one into Ethike's hand, then went away to sit by himself and keep watch while Ethike slept. Ethike didn't immediately go to sleep, though. Agba heard him sniffling and was surprised to see tears leaking from his gaunt face.

Tears are precious, Agba could hear Greatmama say. *Save them, that you may give them to your enemies.*

Agba couldn't decide whether it was good or bad to cry like that. Whether it was a blessing or a curse to have no enemies to give tears to.

*   *   *

The spring was visible before the wagon was. Gushing out of a hole in the sand, its water bubbled up as high as Agba's head. Ethike rushed toward it and fell to his knees, drinking greedily.

Agba, for the first time since he began wandering the desert, felt anger. At that very moment, he could feel The Ogisi's dying breaths deep in the earth below them, just as he watched Ethike thoughtlessly consume Her blood.

It was a different kind of cruelty from the Aleke's. The Aleke's violence was short and swift. This was the cruelty of forgotten transgressions. The cruelty of children absolved of the sins of their parents but never disinherited from their plunders. This cruelty was an evil inscribed into history, so that those who came afterward would know nothing else.

Ethike smiled when he was finished. It was the same smile he always had, but this time Agba found no charm in it.

Are you not thirsty? he asked.

Agba looked away, pretending not to see his hand signs. Eventually, Ethike left, and Agba sat beside the spring alone. He prayed to The Ogisi and asked Her to take care of his greatmama and all the Children, and to keep the memory of Baba firmly in his mind forever.

Only then did he drink, grateful for Her sacrifice.

They spent an entire day sitting in the back of a wagon. During the break, they ate a variety of strange, dried foods he'd never had before, and Agba watched Ethike chew blissfully on the meat of an animal he called a "cow." Agba tried to sleep on the carpeted floor, but it was too rough. Both the soft soil of the Garden and the sand of the desert made for better beds.

The next day, Agba woke to find Ethike smiling over him.

It is not far from here, he signed.

The words were harmless. But as Agba packed supplies and sat on the wagon's lip, looking out at the endlessly rolling hills of sand, the words replayed in his mind.

They reminded Agba of his mission, and he suddenly found it hard to breathe as memories flooded him—memories of Baba's death, of people turned into red splats, of the Aleke's soldiers popping against his palm. Soon, he would be in the City of Lies, and he would have to massacre everyone there. He wasn't ready. He was no warrior, no hero from the stories. He would try to kill one person and he knew the pain would be too much. It would rob him of his consciousness, and the Ajungo would butcher him before he woke.

He just wanted to go home and be out from the desert sun, surrounded by the people who loved him and made sense to him.

Tears welled in his eyes, but no matter how much he recited Great-mama's wisdom and tried to remember Baba's protective arms, the tears wouldn't go away.

Then Ethike was standing in front of him.

Even Gardens have an end, he motioned. *The second Memento of the Ogisi.*

Agba could think of no other meaning to his words but that they were a threat. *Even Gardens have an end.* There was only one Garden. And despite everything the Aleke had done to end it, he had failed. It was Agba who had ended him instead.

That thought calmed him. He had already ended the Aleke. He had avenged Baba. Maybe he could do what had to be done. Maybe he wasn't a hero like Papa Tutu, but he would find a way.

As the pair resumed their journey, Agba said a final prayer to The Ogisi, that She would grant him the strength and the courage to, when the time came, fulfill his mission and wipe every last person in the City of Lies from the world.

✳ ✳ ✳

In short order, walls appeared on the horizon. Agba knew exactly what he was seeing.

The City of Lies.

The walls weren't so tall—a fraction of the size of the Garden's

Great Trees. And they were plain, made from black mud bricks and an iron gate. Yet Ethike began crying again at the sight of them.

Agba wanted to be disgusted. He'd suffered a half dozen stories about the splendor of the city, stories of Ethike's pride in a place responsible for nothing but misery. But he felt no disgust, for he recognized in Ethike the same desire for home that Agba himself felt. He took a step back, unconsciously trying to create a physical distance where he had failed to create an emotional one.

Then there was a loud clanking, and he glanced up to find guards pacing the top of the walls ahead of them. Agba didn't like the way they were looking down at him. With suspicion.

Halt, one of the guards signed. *State your business.*

Ethike had talked enough that Agba knew what his return was supposed to mean. He was supposed to have returned with treasure, not a young boy. Agba also deduced that Ethike was not very powerful in this society. If someone outranking him decided that Agba was to be disposed of, the only way out would be a fight.

Perhaps he was not numb to Ethike, but he cared nothing for these guards. Agba braced himself for battle, readying himself to call upon the Gift.

But he had to be smart. He didn't know how large the city was, how many soldiers it harbored, or what sort of weapons they had. Papa Tutu Himself had fallen to the Ajungo. If Agba hoped to succeed in his mission, he would have to learn more about his enemy.

Only by learning can you free us.

The Ogisi hadn't shown him everything about the City of Lies. He'd thought he was finished learning, but it seemed there was more.

So instead of attacking, Agba continued to play his role. He stepped forward and slipped his hand into Ethike's, the image of the scared little boy Ethike believed him to be. Ethike responded as he always did—a smile. Between the warmth of the smile and the warmth of touching another human for the first time in months, Agba felt a comfort he never thought he'd feel again.

I am Ogisi Ethike, Ethike signed up at the guards. *And I have returned with the treasure from Osi's Tomb.*

The gate glided open, revealing the City of Lies.

Trees with knuckle-bent trunks and great bushy heads were bunched tightly and in abundance, sprouting in rich green between sinewy spires of black brick. Beneath the wind's rustle, Agba could hear the lapping of water and soon spied the reflective glint of a river through the foliage. Birds of every color sailed in flocks above the forest canopy, squawking at the brazen beauty of the day. After weeks of dry desert, the air hung heavy with a refreshing wetness. Agba inhaled as deeply as he could.

It was a garden. Just like home.

In Greatmama's stories, the City of Lies was as harsh and lifeless as the people who lived within it. But this place bore no resemblance to the city Greatmama had told tales of. How could people from such a beautiful place carry such evil within them?

The guards escorted them to what they called the "Capitol," a building that Agba couldn't help but stare up at in wonder. It was like a mushroom overgrown a thousandfold, but designed by people rather than nature. After spiraling up several flights of stairs, they reached a large room with an abundance of sunlight and air flowing through it.

There, iron platters were laid out on a long table. Ethike went immediately over and began eating the offerings, but Agba didn't recognize any of it as food. Fruits and vegetables were food. Nuts and roots were food. The things on the table were unrecognizable—slices of some soft brown rock beside shallow platters piled with white lumps, and a large bowl of what looked to be sand but upon closer inspection was warm and soft to the touch. But he was starving, so he ate what he could, ignoring the foul tastes.

The attendants who took the empty dishes were missing their ears, just like Ethike. In the stories, it was only the soldiers who cut their ears, yet it seemed impossible that soldiers would be used in such a way. There had to be some other reason, one Agba hoped he'd come to understand as he learned more about the city.

Once they finished eating, warm water was brought in porcelain baths. Agba had never seen such a thing, and the idea of dipping himself into warm water—as if he were a bundle of tea leaves—was so absurd that he would have laughed were the situation not so delicate.

So he tried the bath.

It wasn't unpleasant—warm water had its charm.

Finally, once they were bathed and dressed, an attendant said that Ethike was to be taken before the Elders.

I will return, his fingers claimed.

But Agba knew he wouldn't. Since they'd entered the City of Lies, Agba had known his survival was in his own hands. Ethike was an adult, but he understood the world less than Agba did. Agba knew that as soon as Ethike left, the Ajungo would send their soldiers for him. He was from the desert, and anything that came out of the desert knew truths the Ajungo did not want known. They would not risk Agba moving freely through the city.

I told you about my niece, Ethike signed, crouching in front of him so they could see each other eye to eye. *Uwi. You remember?*

Agba nodded.

After this, we will go see her. And you will have someone to play with. How does that sound?

It sounded like something that would never happen; it sounded like something Agba would've enjoyed more than anything else.

As Agba looked into Ethike's eyes, he saw nothing but hope. Sincerity. And he thought about their time together in the desert, how Ethike had fed him and led him to water and shared so many stories of his own life and life in the city. Agba had been taught that stories were special, and that the sharing of a story was a sign of love.

Maybe, Agba thought, Ethike wasn't evil like the Aleke. Maybe he had just been born from evil people, in the same way that Agba had been born from good people.

My name . . . is Agba, he signed.

Ethike embraced him, and Agba again felt comfort. Hugs had been a common part of his day back home. But this hug felt special, like a long draft of water after a month in the desert. He was still a young boy who needed to be loved, and Ethike's love was enough to remind him of his own baba, whose arms had been so sturdy in a world so unstable.

Even water has a story, Ethike said. *The third Memento of the Ogisi. It means that there is always something between the beginning and the end. And that is where life happens. We will live this life together, Agba.*

Then, with a final smile, Ethike was gone.

Agba took a moment to calm himself in the empty room, then he jumped through the nearest window. He used the slightest bit of the Gift to cushion his descent, raising sand up from the ground to catch himself. As he fell, he could feel guards storming into the room he'd just left. Once on the ground, he ran, fleeing from the main roads and plunging into the jungle thicket that stretched across all of the city's untamed parts.

Agba wasn't certain where he would go, but he felt no fear. He would learn all he could about the city and its defenses, and then when the time was right, he would destroy it. He had been born for this purpose, chosen by the Children, chosen by The Ogisi Herself.

It was just a matter of time.

17

AGBA'S PLAN WAS TO live off the land. For weeks, the city's trees would be his home; its fruits would be his meals. All the while, he would observe the people of the City of Lies from afar, plotting his attack.

The first day, he climbed a tree like he had so many times growing up. It was a sprout compared to the Great Trees, but it gave him an elevated view of the city. He watched the people go about their daily routines, leave for work when the sun came up, smile and laugh throughout the day, then return home to their families.

He watched the bakery the most. A bakery, he learned, was a place that made different types of the soft brown rocks Agba had been fed at the Capitol. This specific bakery seemed to be a popular one, and he eventually came to notice their routine of throwing out some of the leftover food each night. He couldn't imagine why anyone would waste food, but he decided to take advantage of it. One evening, he waited until the bakery was closed, then went into the alley behind the store. He retrieved some of the food from a waste bin and bit into the soft cloud of flesh, like spun cotton made food. He chewed for a long while before finally deciding that, despite its strangeness, he enjoyed it.

Agba stalked the bakery for days, rushing in as soon as it closed to gobble up the leftover bread. Each bite was a treat, and he soon came to trust the rats and cats enough to share his banquet with them. The only animals he'd ever seen before were birds and lizards. He'd never seen creatures with hair on their bodies who moved in a careful, thoughtful way—like humans—rather than the sudden, instinctive jerking of the Garden's animals.

He was well into an evening dinner with his new friends when a sound sent the animals scurrying. By the time Agba looked up, someone was already walking toward him down the alley. It was a large man, silhouetted from behind by the moonlight, and for a moment

Agba was convinced it was his baba. Then he remembered that his baba was dead, and so the man in the alley must have been an Ajungo impostor, sent there to confuse and hurt him. The Gift filled him, his skin prickling to life, light swelling against the alley's tight walls. He didn't want to hurt the man, but he would if he had to. He would not let the city destroy him before he destroyed it.

Hello? the man's fingers flashed urgently. *Are you okay?*

It was the baker, Agba realized; his thick forearms and belt-draping belly were unmistakable. Agba had watched the man for over a week. Watched as each day he arrived early to clean the shop before opening to the public. As he kneaded dough of all shapes and sizes, placing them expertly into the oven. And as he smiled at the customers who came and bought from him, as if they were each a beloved family member.

In a way, the man was like Ethike. He seemed kind and gentle. Agba had no desire to hurt him, and if Ethike was any example, maybe he wouldn't have to.

Agba dropped the bread and shied away, releasing the Gift and letting his skin dim.

It is fine, the man signed. He approached Agba and crouched low, just as Ethike had. The adults from the City of Lies seemed to believe that small things were less dangerous. Agba was small, therefore he could not hurt them; they shrank themselves before him, therefore he had to trust them.

Just as he had done with Ethike, Agba reached out his hand, allowing the baker to help him up. The baker took Agba into the bakery's back room and set out some bags of flour behind the oven for Agba to sleep upon. Then he walked to the bakery door, looked back at Agba with pity, and disappeared into the night.

*   *   *

Agba never learned the baker's first name. He introduced himself as Ihenwele and claimed that the bakery had been passed down to him by his greatbaba, who'd passed it down from his greatmama, whose greatmama was the personal baker for Obasa the Wise.

Ihenwele offered Agba the space behind the oven to sleep, and each night he let Agba in and gave him his pick of the leftovers before tossing the rest. That first night, Agba explored the varying basins and bowls and tools arranged carefully about the bakery. After several nights there, he grew comfortable with both the space and Ihenwele.

Like Ethike, Ihenwele told a lot of stories. Stories of days long past, as well as the new stories birthed each day, about an amusing customer or a panicked moment of missing ingredients.

Unlike Ethike, Ihenwele didn't tell his stories from memory. Before each story, he would close his eyes and his skin would flare to life with a million points of dull light. Only when he opened his eyes and his skin returned to normal did he speak.

Agba found the habit unsettling for two reasons. The first was the ghostskin itself. All his life, that pale light had been the uniform of evil. Any attempt to separate the people of the city from the cruelty of their ancestors was spoiled by its appearance. That was why, so long ago, the Children had begun calling them ghosts—that skin was the connection between past and present, the haunting memory of atrocity.

The second reason was simpler: It ruined the stories. Made them feel strange and insignificant. Ethike's stories had felt personal. Great-mama's stories had felt sacred.

Ihenwele's stories felt empty.

You have been here long, the baker once said as he prepared to leave for the evening.

It had been nearly a week, though Agba didn't feel it was especially long—he still hadn't learned much about the city's defenses.

Some of my patrons are aged, Ihenwele continued, and Agba prepared himself for another lengthy story. *They enjoy walking to buy from me, but their children are worried. What if they fall? What if a thief attacks them? I am in need of a runner.*

He paused there, then raised his eyebrows suggestively.

It took Agba a moment to realize what was being asked, but once he did, he couldn't hide the surprise from his face. He'd simply been using the bakery as a place to sleep, leaving as soon as Ihenwele unlocked the door each morning and spending his days watching the city from treetops. He had never considered working there.

But being a runner was a great opportunity to freely explore the city. He would learn far more about its people this way than by hiding in the trees.

Agba nodded. Ihenwele smiled, of course. Just like Ethike.
Good, the baker said. *Tomorrow is on its way.*

*   *   *

Agba was given a daily assignment to deliver bread to three homes.
Two of them were not far from the bakery, but a third took him across
a river to a different part of the city, one where the buildings had a
little more space between them and the trees were small and bore no
fruit. At first, Agba assumed it was a poor area, but Ihenwele explained
that the city's wealthy liked to build homes away from their neighbors
and that their trees were just for decoration, not sustenance.

Once he learned the area was a wealthy one, Agba began to take
extra time during his deliveries. These were the people, he reasoned,
who made the city's decisions. Leaders, generals, important people.
Unlike the other people of the city, who spent their days at work,
these ones were always home, meeting with each other. As far as Agba
could tell, they didn't seem to do much at all, and yet they lived in
the city's most protected area. These were the city's most valuable
members.

It would be a good place to start his attack.

Days became weeks became months. Soon, Agba was delivering
a dozen loaves of bread each morning, all over the city. He drew a
map of everywhere he went, marking important locations—granaries,
bridges, guard barracks—and rushing through his deliveries so that
he could have time to explore more of the city before returning to
the bakery.

Ihenwele hired other children as runners to keep up with increas-
ing demand, and before long they were a fleet of four, including Ihenwele's adopted daughter, Susu. She was smart, and could run nearly
as long and fast as Agba. And she enjoyed teasing him about his ears,
which Agba knew he should have been bothered by, but found he
didn't much mind.

Sit, Agba, Susu signed one afternoon. By then, they were all done
with their deliveries. They always had a few minutes to relax before
Ihenwele put them to work around the store. *Why are you so fast?* she
asked. *Is it because of your small-small legs?*

Agba knew his legs were strong from climbing the Great Trees of
the Garden, but he couldn't say that. He shrugged.

He is not as fast as me, another runner, Yobo, said. He moved to stand beside Susu, leaning against the bakery wall. *Look.* He pulled up the legs of his khaftan to show off his boyish thighs. *You can see muscle, eh?*

Susu rolled her eyes.

Bhune, the fourth runner, said, *What do you want to be, Agba? When you are older.*

Agba had no plans for old age. He hadn't thought a day beyond wiping out the city. He looked away for a moment before responding, pondering which lie to tell.

Agba will be a merchant, Susu interrupted before he could respond. *He will travel all across the Forever Desert.*

I will travel too, Yobo replied. *More than Agba. When I am older, I will be an ogisi. A true ogisi, not like Ethike the Betrayer.*

Agba froze. It had been so long since he'd heard Ethike's name. He thought about the man often, wondering where he had gone and what had become of him.

But Agba couldn't let them know that.

Who is Ethike the Betrayer? he asked.

They had grown used to his questions. He'd told them he'd been born in the western part of the city, which was more rural and less informed. That had been enough for them to not think him strange when he asked about things that were commonplace to them.

Bhune pulled a pamphlet from his delivery bag. Agba had seen such newsletters around town, but since he couldn't read, he'd never had reason to inspect them further.

The new issue of The Speaker *tells everything,* Bhune said with his free hand.

Read it to us, Susu said.

Susu had no trouble reading. She'd asked entirely for Agba's sake.

Bhune summarized the story for them. Ethike, the ogisi who had left the city nearly a year before on the royal quest, had returned. Except he had tried to betray the city by selling information about Obasa's Tomb to other cities of the Forever Desert. He had been stripped of his title and the Great Temple of Osi was being converted to a gymnasium.

"It is not true," Agba said aloud to himself.

In his months in the city, he had begun to think in their signed language rather than his own tongue. But in that moment, all the care and calm he'd crafted to survive in the city was burned away. Ethike was no traitor. The only thing he was guilty of, Agba knew, was telling the truth about the Garden and what they were doing to the Children.

There is no tomb, Agba signed. The other runners were nice people. Maybe they were from the City of Lies, but he knew the truth was important to them. *There is only people. The Children of Tutu. Your Aleke cuts off the Children's hands and ties them around their necks as a reminder to submit to his rule. He has done this for centuries. That is what Ogisi Ethike learned, and now the Elders are punishing him.*

Agba found his hands were shaking by the end, so much that he wasn't sure they had even understood his signing. They all looked at him, silent.

Then each of them closed their eyes, and their skin flared to life, and Agba stared in bewilderment as his fellow runners all seemed lost in a trance.

Then they opened their eyes and their skin dimmed.

No, that is wrong, Agba, Bhune said first. *The Aleke is only a farmer.*

The ogisi do not do that, Yobo added. *The ones who leave the city die in the desert.*

Where did you learn such a tale? Susu laughed. *The Elders do not punish ogisi.*

They continued discussing Ethike and *The Speaker* and their future aspirations.

Agba sat wordlessly beside them, fighting the tears that stung his eyes.

Tears are precious.

There was nothing he could say to them. So long as the people of the City of Lies could retreat into the false stories of their ghostskins, they would never be able to understand the world beyond their walls. The Gift that he had been given to save his people was the same power that allowed the people of the City of Lies to remain ignorant of his people's plight.

But why?

The Ogisi gave Her Gift to all who prayed to Her, yet these people did not pray. The Ogisi had given Her Gift to Agba for his mission, yet these people had no missions. He didn't understand how The Ogisi could look upon these people, see the pain they had caused, and still grant them power. She desired creation; they did nothing but destroy. They had corrupted Her divine power—fouling it, distorting it, using it to bring an endless stream of lies into the world.

There had to be an explanation. There had to be something he was missing.

That night, and many after, he prayed for understanding.

And The Ogisi answered his prayer.

With silence.

18

THERE IS A LONELINESS that comes from being alone; there is a loneliness that comes from being with others.

Agba tried over and over to tell his fellow runners about a world they didn't know. At first, they would slip into their ghostskins and return with a truth that negated anything he was saying. But as his desperation increased, they no longer bothered with using their ghostskins. They just ignored him.

Even Susu.

Further rumors about Ethike, spurred by *The Speaker*'s wild accusations, isolated Agba from the others even more. ETHIKE THE BE-TRAYER INVESTIGATED FOR TREASON. ETHIKE THE BETRAYER KEEPS A CHILD SLAVE. ETHIKE THE BETRAYER SENTENCED TO IMPRISONMENT; CITY REJOICES. In just a few weeks, Ethike became the enemy of the people, and any attempt Agba made to defend him only made the others dislike him more.

He had never felt so lonely.

One day, Agba was sitting by the front entrance of the bakery, watching the other runners converse a dozen strides away, when he felt a tap on his back. He turned to find Ihenwele standing over him.

Come with me, he signed.

Ihenwele led Agba away from the others and into the bakery's back room. There, he poured flour, water, milk, and yeast into a large tin bowl and began mixing it. It was strange, seeing hands used in this way. For most of his life, Agba had only ever seen hands used by the Aleke and his friends to communicate. Since coming to the city, he'd seen hands used for all manner of things—pushing and pulling and tying and grabbing.

But this was different. There was care here, a gentle power. For some reason, as Ihenwele kneaded the mix into a thick dough, Agba missed his baba. Baba would have made such great use of hands if he'd had them. Maybe he even would have learned to make bread, and every morning Agba would have risen to the warm scent of freshly baked loaves.

After some time, Ihenwele stepped back from the brown dough, leaving it sitting on the counter.

What are you doing? Agba asked. His job as a runner meant that by the time the bread got to him, it was fully baked; he'd never seen the bread-making process before.

Ihenwele leaned back against the counter. *Waiting,* he signed.

What should I do?

Learn.

Agba didn't know what he was supposed to be learning.

How long will you wait?

Until it is ready.

Over the next hour or so, Ihenwele cleaned some of the dirty mixing tins, spent some time recording numbers in his ledger, distributed loaves of bread for the other runners to take into town, and ignited the fire in the brick oven. Any time Agba asked what he could do, Ihenwele's response was the same.

Learn.

By the time the baker returned to the dough, it had swelled to nearly thrice the size it had been before.

How did you do that? Agba asked.

It was not me.

Agba frowned, confused. *The bread made itself bigger?*

Ihenwele glanced at him, amused. *The baker does not make the bread. He feeds the bread what it needs—water, yeast, heat.*

Then what?

Then trust. Do what you can do, trust what you must trust. Whether yeast, an oven, or others.

Ihenwele jabbed his head in the direction of the front entrance, toward where the other runners so often stood.

Agba understood. Ihenwele was right. He was a wise man, worth listening to. But something in Agba was mistrustful, and a question that started in the back of his mind had worked its way to the front by the time the sun had fallen and the day was at its end.

Do you believe me? Agba asked.

The other runners were gone. It was just Ihenwele and Susu, the latter waiting outside for her baba. Together, Agba and Ihenwele had finished cleaning the kitchen as they did every night, and Ihenwele was ready to leave.

Believe you? the baker asked.

Believe me about Ethike and the Children.

Ihenwele smiled.

Then his skin erupted with tiny points of iridescence, every pore alight. When he returned to normal, he simply pinched Agba's nose, then turned to leave the bakery.

Rest well, Agba. Tomorrow is on its way, he signed before closing the door behind him.

✳   ✳   ✳

Ihenwele made Agba a full-time apprentice. Gone were Agba's days of exploring the city. Instead, his life was confined to the kitchen. To flour and rolling pins, cool water and hot ovens. The work was hard at first—Agba didn't know his arms could be so sore.

But months passed.

Then years.

And soon, Agba found himself counted among the most skilled bakers in the city. He'd wake at first light and get to work so that by the time Ihenwele arrived, much of the baking was done. Ihenwele would taste the first batch and offer either a quick shake of his head or a blissful nod. The highs and lows of Agba's days all became centered around bread. Only in that sliver of time between the last batch and the nightly cleaning did he take a break. He'd briefly watch patrons or look out the window at the runners. However, he rarely spoke to customers and never spoke to the runners. The baking kept his days busy and brought him a sense of satisfaction, but it wasn't enough.

At night, long after Ihenwele had left, Agba would sneak out of the bakery to continue work on his map of the city. It was harder at night, but after a long day inside, he didn't mind spending extra hours in a tree to sketch out the shadowed details of one neighborhood or another. His forays taught him everything there was to learn about the City of Lies. Its nine districts and three rivers; its west-side livestock and east-side commerce; its sunken iron mines and soaring Great Temples.

And its people. He hid in bushes and peered into windows, watching families enjoy dinner, siblings play fight, couples resting their heads together. Often, someone's eyes would go distant and their skin would sparkle. There was much of that. People lying in bed with skin sparkling when they could have been sleeping. Parents lost in the power of The Ogisi while their children played recklessly before them.

In his observing the city, Agba came to see the deep contradictions in the hearts of her people. They considered themselves good, yet not a second of their days was spent wondering about the evils committed in their name. They revered the dead king Obasa for his wisdom, yet few of them sought wisdom for themselves. They called themselves a city of stories, yet they cut away their ears so that they could not hear the stories of others.

They were capable of great love and mercy, the people of the City of Lies. Agba saw this a thousand times over: the adoration in the eyes of a greatbaba as he held his greatchild for the first time; the selfless shooing of a shopkeeper refusing to accept payment from a patron on her last coin. Yet they were also capable of a unique and terrible cruelty that they weren't even aware of. A cruelty, in fact, that only survived through their inability to see it.

∗   ∗   ∗

By the time Agba completed his map of the city, he was in his early twenties. He was tall, though not much taller than the average citizen of the city, and was all lean muscle from his nights climbing trees. He grew out his hair so that he could hide his ears whenever he needed to go among the people.

When he looked at the map—the map he'd begun as a child, lost and lonely in a foreign land—a tumult arose in him. On it was labeled every barracks and watchtower and armory. Every warehouse full of grain, every furrowed farm. It was a key to the city's destruction, yet he no longer sought to use it. His hatred for the people of the city had dissolved as his familiarity with them grew.

There was still, however, the Ajungo.

In the years that passed, there was little news of Ethike. Agba doubted the man was still alive, but if he was, it must have been in a city dungeon. The Ajungo had destroyed the man's name and livelihood—it wasn't hard to believe they would end his life if they felt it would further their aims. If Agba wanted to save the Children, he wouldn't need to destroy the whole city. He would just need to destroy the Ajungo.

His plan for that was close to fruition.

Uncle Agba, Keze's fingers signed in front of his face. *We are late.*

Agba leaned back from the ledger, exhaling himself out of his thoughts and back into the real world. His back was stiff from bending over the bakery counter, his eyes weary from triple checking the day's figures. Ihenwele had made Agba the manager after opening another bakery across the city, which meant Agba was responsible for everything from the baking to the customers to hiring new runners.

Thank you, he signed back. The wall clock said ten past the hour—they were indeed late. *Let's clean up and be away. Quick.*

Keze was the first runner he'd hired, and she had been a trusty assistant since. Together, they cleaned up and closed down the bakery for the night, and then they were on their way.

In his decade in the city, Agba had never been to a Silencing. Silencings were usually intimate family things, and he had no intimate family in the city. Which was why he'd been both surprised and grateful when Susu—his brief childhood friend and the heir to the growing Ihenwele bakery empire—had invited him to the Silencing of her first child.

Beneath the wide branches of the neighborhood talking tree, shaded against the joyful evening sun, an assembly stood.

Closest to the tree's trunk was the young couple, Susu and her husband, the flush of love still in their faces and a babe in Susu's arms. An older woman dressed in the attire of the city's so-called ogisi stood beside the couple, a waist-high basin of water. As Agba and Keze arrived, heads turned to acknowledge them. Nods and smiles were exchanged.

The ogisi was in the middle of a speech about the history of the ritual. How Obasa had given it to the people of the city as a way to protect them. How it was the only thing keeping them safe from the Ajungo's deadly song.

After the speech, the ogisi took the baby and raised him high for all to see. There is a perfection in babies that exists nowhere else in nature, and Susu's baby was no different. Plump and sleepy, bald as a sweet plum. Agba thought back with shame on how, over the years, he had let their childhood awkwardness keep them apart. Susu had created something beautiful, and no one capable of such beauty could be so bad.

Then the ogisi plunged the baby into the water.

The Silencing ritual was no secret. Agba had known what to expect. Still, seeing a newborn plunged into frigid waters is a sight not done justice by stories. Each passing second with the child submerged was elongated into the arrhythmic timescale of nightmares. Agba was a child again, adrift in the black uncertainty of the Garden's pond. Were he not paralyzed by shock, he would have leapt forward to yank the child out, but all he could make himself do was pray for The Ogisi to intervene and save the child from this false prophet.

By the time the baby was removed, he was limp. His skin was tinged blue beneath its paleness. Dead.

Then the child began to shine.

Light from within leaked out from the child's every pore, dull and white but unmistakably identical to the power of The Ogisi. The baby coughed, expelling spouts of water. Its cries rippled the air with a frantic and gurgling desperation.

A cry none of them could hear, Agba realized

The ogisi placed the baby on a nearby table, produced a blade and, with all the indifference of parting dough, chopped down, shearing the baby's ears from its head. She drew a hot iron rod from a pot beside her, and its flat end flared hotly before she placed it against the gaping wound. Burning flesh didn't smell so bad as rotting flesh. But the sound—a growing hiss punctuated with bulbous pops as flesh overheated and burst—was one he would remember as long as he lived.

The onlooking adults had their arms in the air, hands waving rapidly, feet pounding. They were exuberant. The baby's uncles and aunties, Yobo and Bhune, the entire community. They were all smiling and celebrating. They were happy.

Even Ihenwele. Agba had never seen such unrestrained joy on the baker's face. Tears glittered in his eyes, rolled down the smiling lines of his face to slip off the edge of his lips—lips that quivered with emotion. One arm grabbed his wife in an embrace, the other shook hands proudly with the various uncles who ambled over to congratulate him. He kept shaking his head, so overwhelmed by the beauty of the moment that he had to deny it.

Susu beamed with pride. She and her husband pressed their heads together, gazing with love at their screaming baby wrapped in blood-soaked cloth. *His first Sight,* she signed.

Time moves differently in the desert. There are no mountains to accumulate and shed snows, no trees that cycle through colors, no rivers that dry up and overflow. It wasn't until he arrived at the city that Agba first learned of clocks. The first time he heard a clock ticking and watched its hands crawl around its face, time that had otherwise been static for most of his life now had a rhythm. Click. Click. Click. He was charmed and horrified to find it often synced with his heartbeat. He'd never noticed his heartbeat much before. In the Garden, there was always someone talking somewhere, a voice that drew his attention. But the silence of the City of Lies had introduced Agba to clocks alongside the beating of his heart, a merging of the natural and unnatural.

As Susu and Ihenwele and all their family celebrated the maiming of their child, Agba could hear only the clicking of his heart. The rhythm of time that stretched from his first breath in the Garden to that very moment. For years, he'd been asking why The Ogisi gave her power to these people—these descendants of Papa Tutu's enemies. Now he had his answer.

They weren't being given the Gift.

It was the water.

It had always been the water.

Even water has a story.

Ethike hadn't realized the wisdom that had been passed down to him. The entire history of the world, condensed into three sayings. Mementos, he'd called them. Every answer to every question, simpler than could be imagined.

Only by learning can you free us.

Over the years, Agba had come to believe that perhaps there was a life for him other than vengeance. A life of creation rather than destruction. He had truly come to believe that these people were good, that perhaps it was just their leaders who were cruel.

He had done the one thing he had been asked not to do. He had *forgotten.*

His eyes grew heavy with the threat of tears.

Tears are precious . . .

He left the assembly, disregarding the stares and inquiring hands reaching after him. His eyes burned as he dazed his way back to the bakery, where he fell into the same corner he'd first slept in a decade before.

. . . *save them* . . .

He wanted nothing more than to weep. But he couldn't.

Not yet.

. . . *that you may give them to your enemies.*

19

THE ASCENDANCE WAS AN old holiday that marked the first day of spring. There was no bigger celebration in the City of Lies. It began with an address from the Elders at the Capitol, and all the city's most powerful merchants, generals, and ogisi were in attendance.

All Agba's targets together in one spot.

Over the years, he had snuck into the Capitol several times to work on his map, and he'd had no difficulty doing so again, especially under the cover of night. He slipped past the exterior pillars and over to the central base, where he found a closet on the ground floor. It was narrow and deep, but so filled with brooms and buckets and washcloths that Agba barely had anywhere to sit. In a sense, he found it fitting that he would start his attack from so lowly a place. Let the Ajungo's downfall forever be their disregard for those below them.

In the hours that passed, as he sat in the thick dark of the room, Agba prayed to Papa Tutu. For years, Papa Tutu had been the only person he could talk to. The Ogisi was distant and unknowable, but Papa Tutu had been human, like him, and understood the burden of power. Agba didn't pray for anything specific—it was the act of prayer itself that brought him peace, to know he was a child of the divine and to feel the conviction of his purpose. The evil of the Ajungo was the scourge of history. They did not deserve kindness. They did not deserve life. And Agba would end them here, now and forever.

But the Ajungo, he'd learned, were the leaders their people deserved. They were just as callous and cruel as the tailors and bakers, merchants and physicians, greatmamas and greatbabas of the City of Lies. He had told them the truth and they'd ignored it. He'd begged them to listen and they had refused. Even Ihenwele.

Do what you can do, trust what you must trust.

Ihenwele—all of them—had chosen the comforting stories of their minds rather than face the cruelties of their empire. If he killed the

Ajungo, new leaders from among the same corrupted peoples would simply rise to take their place.

Every last one had to be wiped away. Let it all begin anew.

The closet door opened, and dim light flooded in.

The old man who entered went about his work without a single glance in Agba's direction. His fingers were knobbed and misshapen from a life of physical labor, his back curled as if hunched away from a raised fist. His hair was receded to a thin rim along the sides of his head.

He reached to grab a broom handle that was a mere stride from Agba's face, and as Agba got a good look at the man's hands, they tugged at his memories.

They were the first pair of hands he'd ever seen up close.

"Ethike . . ." he muttered.

The old man didn't react, unable to see Agba even from arm's length away. Then Agba took a step forward, emerging into the light.

There was no startle. Just a moment of confusion before a burst of recognition. Ethike threw his arms in the air, his mouth a tall oval, his eyebrows two high arches. In that moment, he looked young again, and whole, the brave explorer on the verge of the biggest discovery of his life.

The next moment, all his features collapsed—arms and mouth and eyebrows buckling again to the weight of time. It was a warm day, yet Ethike's body trembled as if his blood was ice. Tears leaked from his wide, unblinking eyes. His jaw hung loose, with gaps in place of teeth, like broken windows on a disused building.

Agba . . . Ethike's fingers shook so much Agba could barely understand him. *You are alive.*

Agba closed the door and helped Ethike sit on an overturned bucket. Above and around them, the volume of the crowd was growing. The Ascendance would begin soon.

I thought about you every day, Ethike eventually signed. *When you disappeared, I thought it was the Elders who took you, and I kept asking and asking. I told them that if they did not return you . . .*

Ethike the fool. He had walked into the jaws of a lion and tried to tell it what to eat.

The Ajungo imprisoned him. Defamed him to the public. The

torture Ethike described was soul-spilling. They broke his mind and body, rebuilt him into something they could force into servanthood with an assurance he would never act against them. Ethike had joined history's infinite line of the oppressed, those whose voices were so dangerous they were taken from them by force.

But you are here, Ethike concluded. *You are here. Why?*

A question. How long had it been since anyone in this city had asked Agba a question rather than seek the answer themselves in the foul slip of their ghostskins? There was anticipation in Ethike's eyes, a thirst for explanation. Hope.

I am here to destroy the city, Ethike, Agba replied. He didn't relish wiping the expression from the man's face.

Ethike's gaze was searching, as if Agba's words would eventually expose themselves as a joke. Then, understanding.

It was you . . . he signed. *In the desert, all those years ago.* Sweat materialized along the remnants of his hairline. *The Ajungo.*

Agba frowned, certain Ethike had misunderstood. *What?*

The rage of the Forever Desert, Ethike signed. *The Ajungo.*

In other circumstances, Agba would've laughed at the irony. All his life, his people had lived in fear of the Ajungo across the desert. It seemed that Ethike's people had as well.

Ethike actually did laugh. Despite the smoke and blood of his torture-ravaged throat, Ethike's laugh was clean, pure joy. He didn't sign his laughter. It was just the sound, one that only Agba could hear. A private thing for the two of them to enjoy.

Then the sound of laughter cut off, and there was a gradual slide from mirth to tears. Ethike covered his mouth behind his hands, but his unblocked eyes were wet and trembling and full of something that Agba remembered seeing in the desert all those years ago.

Pity.

What have we taken from you? Ethike asked as the tears pooled and dribbled down his cheeks.

Here was a man not yet fifty whose youth had been stolen. His hair, teeth, and dignity all in shambles. He had been stripped of title and land, his reputation dissolved. His very freedom yanked from his hands. Yet it was Agba he pitied.

For ten years, Agba explained, *I have lived among your people. I have seen that you are all capable of great love, for each other and for your city. Yet I have also seen an ignorance so vile it outweighs all else. You think yourself a city of stories, but my greatmamas named you rightly—you are indeed a city of lies.*

Outside, there was a surge of sound, as of a thousand hands clapping at once.

The Ascendance had begun.

And so you would kill us all? Ethike replied. *Not just the Elders, but our merchants and blacksmiths? Cleaners and stable hands? You would punish the innocent for their proximity to the guilty?*

Agba shook his head. *There are no innocents.*

He explained everything. Shokolokobangoshe and the creation of the desert. The Garden and the Aleke. The Ogisi and the Gift and how the people of the City of Lies had come by their power.

The water.

When he was finished, Ethike's face was flat with disbelief. *Even deserts have a beginning,* the former ogisi signed to himself. *Even gardens have an end. Even water has a story.*

It is Her blood that allows humans to See as She does, Agba signed. *But we are not gods. We cannot See as gods do. As long as there is water to drink, your people will use lies to destroy mine. I was sent here to end this.*

Many times over the years Agba had told his story. And every time he had been met with cold skepticism.

In Ethike, there was warm understanding. Sorrow. Shame. Regret. Belief.

In shock, Agba sought the protective power of the Gift. He became wreathed in scales of light, an image of The Ogisi Herself. His body expanded—not in size, but in awareness. Everything around him became an extension of himself, from within the small closet to across the city. The Capitol above him could be moved with the bend of his neck. The river to the east was his arm made liquid.

Remember Ogisi, the voices of the Children whispered to him.

He was ready.

The stables will have extra camels today, Agba signed. *Take one and ride out of the city as hard as you can.*

I cannot simply leave.

Why? Agba replied with a bite he couldn't suppress. *You have no leash. They have not cut off your hands and wrapped them around your throat.*

Ethike looked away for so long that Agba thought he might have fallen asleep. But when he turned back, his tears had dried, and his face was set with resolve.

Please, he signed with a final desperation, *before you do this, allow me to tell you one last story.*

*   *   *

Agba felt like a child again, sitting at Greatmama's feet and listening to her tales. It had been ten years. Greatmama was likely dead by now. He wouldn't hear her stories anymore.

This city was destroyed once before, Ethike began. *There is only one account of the event, as I suspect the histories were purged. It was called the Night of the Rising Sun, and it was the night Obasa the Bloody—as the source calls him—took the city. He killed over half the population and enslaved most of the rest. It was retaliation, for all the evils the leaders of the city had perpetrated against his people. That same murderous man became forever known as Obasa the Wise. History is only a story, after all.*

Agba was still filled with the power of the Gift. It itched beneath his skin, hungry for release.

I tell you this, Ethike continued, *because I want you to know that the path you walk has been walked before. You will wipe out Obasa's legacy, as Obasa wiped out those before him. And when you are old, or perhaps after you have rejoined your ancestors, you will watch your legacy be wiped away by the next conqueror, who will retaliate against your people for what you do this day.*

You are correct, Agba signed. *Which is why I must leave no one to retaliate.*

Please. Ethike's signing took on greater urgency. *My niece, Uwi. Do you remember her?*

Agba had never met her. All he knew about the girl were the stories Ethike had told.

She works in the records office, Ethike added. *Two floors above us. If you do this, you will kill her along with the rest of us.* Ethike pursed his parched lips and looked very much the image of a heartbroken parent, one who had failed to protect their child.

Then he closed his eyes.

At first, Agba thought Ethike had resigned himself to death. But there was a deep, unflinching serenity in his face. It was confidence, not resignation. The peace of the victorious warrior, not the submission of the defeated one. Ethike was not afraid to die.

Agba signed, thinking the aged scholar would open his eyes to see. No. He tapped Ethike on the knee to no response.

"Open your eyes," Agba said. He had so rarely used his voice over the last decade, yet the inclination still remained.

When Ethike's eyes remained closed, Agba spoke anyway.

"When I was sent here, I was told to make them remember. For ten long years, I have failed to make you all listen, much less remember. Now I am here on the precipice of fulfilling my purpose, and you would have me stop. What happens when the next ogisi goes out into the desert in search of Osi's Tomb? What happens when this ogisi meets my people and finds what the Aleke found? If you could remember the things I remember, you would not be so forgiving."

Ethike heard none of it. Yet, somehow, eyes still firmly shut, he responded.

Even deserts have a beginning, he signed. *Even gardens have an end. Even water has a story.*

It was that, of all things, that changed Agba's mind.

If Ethike could remember the things Agba could remember, he wouldn't change at all. He would be just as forgiving. Not because he was a fool. But because he had faith in people, no matter that they might hurt him, no matter that they might humiliate him, no matter how many times they failed him.

And by closing his eyes, Ethike was placing his faith in Agba.

Ethike was a decent person. The one decent person in the entire City of Lies.

Agba had thought the Three Mementos of the Ogisi were a coded history of the Forever Desert, a revelation of truth. But in that moment, on the cusp of destroying the City of Lies and its people, he realized it held no code at all. It was a simple message of faith. Of hope.

Learn well, my son. Only by learning can you free us.

Ten years ago, Agba had been on a mission to destroy the City of Lies. But he'd learned so much since then. So, so much.

"I see," Agba said.

I see, Agba signed.

20

AGBA STOOD BEFORE the Ajungo.

In the stories, they were shadowed and powerful, unseen and cruel. In life, they were just old men and women—their faces wrinkled, their spirits withered, their appetites for power insatiable. Agba had never expected this day to come. As a child, the thought of confronting them had terrified him. He'd planned to destroy the Capitol without ever seeing them in person. Now, he couldn't imagine having gone his whole life without meeting his enemies face-to-face.

Behind them, water fell from the ceiling into the floor in an endless loop.

What have you come here for, they asked in synchronized signs, *Child of the Desert?*

"I come on behalf of The Ogisi," Agba said aloud. "And as the chosen son of the Children of Tutu."

He'd spent hours discussing with Ethike, during which the Ascendence had ended and the people of the city had returned to their homes. Ethike had urged nonviolence, and Agba listened to his counsel. Ultimately, they had agreed on a solution Agba had encountered before but had not believed possible. Now, because of Ethike, it was.

"I offer you a deal," Agba continued. "You do not yet know this, but your city is in need of peace. A peace I alone can offer you."

All around him, Agba could feel the Ajungo's soldiers. They were hiding behind pillars, in dark corners of the ceiling, even on the floor below.

"And what is the price of your peace?" one of the Ajungo responded aloud.

"Water," Agba replied, and he was unsurprised by their laughter. "You will give me all of your city's water, and in exchange I will give you a peace that your greatchildren will not see the end of."

"And if we decline?"

Agba took a deep breath. "For your sake and the sake of your descendants," he said, "choose peace."

But he knew they wouldn't. Agba had spent the last decade having his honesty rejected by the people of the City of Lies. They knew too much and were too certain in their knowledge. The Ajungo were no different.

"We must decline your offer," one of them said.

"You mustn't."

"We do not know you. We do not trust you."

"Of course you do not trust me," Agba replied. "You think I am the monster from a garden in the desert. Yet, to me, it is you who is that monster. This cycle of death and oppression does not persist because we fail to learn from it. But because we are each of us monsters born into gardens, and we all fear being thrust into the harshness of the desert.

"So do not trust me," Agba implored, "but trust that I fear that desert as much as you. And would do anything in my power to avoid it."

The Ajungo were quiet then, though not because they were weighing his words or silently deliberating. They were simply waiting for their soldiers to reach their positions.

"We represent our people," they eventually said. "As you represent yours. And our people cannot survive if they don't have water."

"And my people cannot survive if they do," Agba whispered.

He had told Ethike that this was how it would end. Ethike had refused to believe, of course. It was worth a try.

And Agba had tried.

The Ajungo's soldiers sprung their trap, attacking from every direction, human-shaped masses of light collapsing on Agba.

Agba used the Gift.

All of the city was an extension of his body. He turned his head and a wall of the Capitol collapsed, sunlight slashing across the room. He raised his toes and the left side of the building fell away like a mudslide. He closed his fingers into a fist and the world began drawing into him, swelling him beyond the limits of his body, the fabric of the City of Lies melding into the hot glow of his skin.

In seconds, his head was bursting through the ceiling, and he looked down to find a body made of sand hundreds of strides high. The Ajungo—the most powerful leaders in the history of the world—were blood spatters far below him, scarcely recognizable among the sand and brick and wood surging into his ever-growing body. The soldiers continued to attack, just as the Aleke's had. They fought bravely, but Agba extinguished them by the dozens, and for a few seconds blood and flesh rained from the sky, their iron weapons clattering to the ground below.

Each death pained him, but he remained conscious. He had never managed to completely numb himself. Perhaps he was grateful for that. The soldiers were a necessary sacrifice, the only thing left that could stop Agba and Ethike from achieving the peace they planned, but he did not want to feel nothing for his foes. He'd seen in the Aleke the folly of true numbness.

With the Ajungo slain, the Capitol destroyed, and its soldiers defeated, Agba ceased drawing in the city's sand and brick and trees.

Instead, he drew in its water. Three rivers became one, burrowing through neighborhoods in waves twenty feet high, erasing homes and the doomed souls within them, sluicing across valleys to convene on him. The earth where the Capitol used to be raised up, detonating all the surrounding buildings in a violent cloud of dust and bone and screams. It formed into a plateau as high as any mountain, and into it he poured all of the city's water—every last drop of moisture whisked from every slick fish and fat root—until the city's healthy soil was as dry and brittle as the sand of the desert. Then he sealed it.

Finally, when it was finished, Agba released the Gift and sat upon the reservoir of his own making. There, having finally given tears to his enemies, he wept.

21

AFTER THE SILENCING OF Susu's child, Agba had wandered the City of Lies. Not to continue mapping it, nor to take a final tour of the foods he would miss; not to visit some of his favorite animal friends, nor to visit customers from his old bread delivery route.

But to beg.

He started at busy intersections, standing atop a wooden box with his hands high. The passersby mostly ignored him, but the town Peacekeepers threatened him with arrest, so he moved on. Outside the university, students were more willing to engage than most. They'd stop and listen, but ultimately he would say something that seemed untrue to them and they would consult their ghostskin before walking away. Agba went on to the markets, where he was ignored, the garment district, where he was ridiculed; and to the Great Temples, where he'd hoped the ogisi's aversion to the Gift would help them heed his words. Instead, they challenged him to provide evidence for his claims, books by reputable scholars, letters from original sources.

Of course, there were no books for his claims—he was simply telling his story. When he pulled back his mangy thicket of hair to show his ears, they claimed a small percentage of families refused to enter into the Silence, and that he was likely a child of such a family. When he offered to show them with Sight, they said his Sight would be no better than any random citizen's. When he told them he was a personal friend of Ethike, they laughed, or grew quiet and walked hurriedly away.

The people began calling him a heretic, then they began calling him *the* Heretic, and then they began treating him like a heretic. When he told them of the Garden, he was jeered. When he explained the Children, people hurled stones at him. At mention of the Aleke, and what the ogisi were doing, he was spit on, covered in refuse, jailed.

At any point, he could have used the Gift. However, Agba had decided to give the people of the City of a Thousand Stories a final chance to spare themselves. He remembered everything they had done to the Children, everything The Ogisi had shown him. Yet he still did not believe the city's people had to die, and if he could find a single decent person—just one who would hear his story and believe—he would find another way.

He eventually took his ministry to the taverns. He'd be out well into the night, to when even the most loyal drunkards were ready to go home. He hadn't expected them to be any more receptive than their sober countrymen, but they were far worse. He was attacked on two occasions, once being beaten to near unconsciousness before they relented. But he went back every day for weeks, signing for any who would stop and watch.

And one night, someone did. He was a regular, a beggar who sat outside the tavern twice a week, hoping a drunk would pity him. He had ignored Agba every other day, going to the other side of the bar to beg so as to not compete for attention. But that night, the beggar left his usual corner and stood in front of Agba on swaying legs, watching his every word. Agba told him of the Garden, and of the Children, and of the Aleke and the ogisi, and the beggar did not interject.

Do you understand? Agba asked when he finished.

For the first time, it seemed that someone did. The beggar did not slip into his ghostskin, nor accuse Agba of lying or delusion. He just listened.

Agba had found his decent person.

You the Heretic? the beggar responded.

I am Agba of the Garden, from the Forever Desert.

The beggar eyed him. *You don't take money?*

I am here to give, not receive.

And what is it you're giving?

The truth.

The beggar waved his hand by his mouth, laughing. *Well, there's your problem.*

Problem?

You're trying to give something you don't have.

Agba felt a pained wind escape his lips. Another naysayer. There was not a single soul in the wretched city worth saving, from top to bottom, kings to beggars.

The truth is no camel, Heretic, the beggar continued. *Nobody owns it. All you have is a story. They get to decide if it's true or not. Like me.* He sat down with his back against the tavern wall, then slumped until his posture was truly horrendous. *This is how I do it. I even hide an arm, make them think it's lost. That's my story—the one-armed beggar.*

So you're a beggar and a liar, Agba shot back.

At that, the man's whole demeanor changed. He sat up, adjusted his tattered khaftan, and ran a hand over his hair. His wide, unruly features seemed to draw together, controlled and pointed.

Just as your truth is a story, so are my lies. And my story puts these clothes on my back. My story feeds my children. What has your story gotten you but spit on? He rose on unsteady legs, and with a final acidic stare, said: *Better a beggar and a liar than a beggar and a fool.*

With that, he strode into the night.

Agba stayed outside the tavern for another hour. He didn't stand on his wooden box, didn't sign his story to anyone. He just sat on the road, gaze unfocused, hands at his side. The beggar's insults clung to his thoughts. Part of him wondered if perhaps his mission to spread the truth was a selfish one. If, perhaps, there was a lie that would have better protected the Children. Not a lie. A story.

But a larger part of him knew they wouldn't listen to such a story anyway. He had searched for just one decent person among them. One person who proved capable of believing, who could prove that there was hope for these people. He hadn't found it. The City of Lies deserved no stories.

22

THERE IS NO WATER in the *City of Lies*.

This was the first story that Agba and Ethike had crafted. It was the water that gave people knowledge, and the knowledge that corrupted them. There would be those who remembered. Who knew how absurd it was that a city once flourishing with life had been reduced to a dust-choked desert. Who remembered the name the city had given itself rather than the name Agba had imposed upon it. And so the punishment for any who defied this story would be the loss of their hands, ensuring that they could not spread their dissent to others. To Ethike, it was a monstrous punishment; to Agba, more merciful than they deserved. Eventually—in short time, they both hoped—the story would be accepted, just as so many stories before it had been, and the people would preserve it themselves.

Agba sat at the wagon's reins. A decade had passed since his defeat of the Ajungo, and the City of Lies was pacified enough that he had decided to return to the desert. In Agba's time governing the city, Ethike had taught him of the wider world. There were other cities with other people claiming to be ogisi. Those cities would continue to send new ogisi to the Garden.

Which meant the Children of Tutu still weren't free.

Safe journey, Ethike signed. He had healed greatly from what the Ajungo had done to him, but he still appeared older than his years, the memory of pain burned into him for the rest of his days. In Agba's absence, Ethike would govern the city.

Beside him was his heir, Uwi, now a brilliant and bright-eyed woman. The years had been unkind to Ethike and Uwi's relationship. Whereas Ethike could forgive the city for what it had done to him, Uwi had watched her uncle suffer with a simmering desire for vengeance. It had been that, far more than games and food, that she and Agba eventually bonded over.

When Ethike and Agba discussed the future of the city, they both concluded that Uwi was the only one suited to truly lead. She possessed a violent intolerance toward injustice that Ethike lacked, and a love of the city and its people that Agba could never feel. Agba told her his story and the many painful stories of the Forever Desert. He used the Gift to show her what suffering looked like beyond the bounds of her time and land. He had made her smell decaying hands, taste the ash of vengeful fires. And she had come to agree that peace was worth protecting, for it was always better than its alternatives.

The Silence has ended, Ethike had pointed out. *The language of the tongue has already begun to spread again through our city. The cutting of hands will not work forever.*

Uwi had leveled at her uncle a stone-eyed look. *Then we cut their tongues.*

Ethike had been aghast; Agba, grateful—Uwi was their only hope for a future that avoided the folly of the past. The second story they crafted would secure that future:

There are no heroes in the City of Lies.

Agba knew well the brutality of drought. He was not unsympathetic to the suffering he was creating, but he knew it to be a lesser suffering than all that had come before. Suffering always birthed aspiring heroes who sought to relieve it—he himself had been one. The only way to prevent that was to make a world without heroism. One in which suffering is to be accepted, not fought.

After double-checking his map and the camels, Agba nodded to both Ethike and Uwi. He did not know whether he would ever see them again. The Forever Desert was larger than could be easily conceived, and he couldn't say how many years it would take him to find and defeat the leaders of its other cities.

Be well, my friends, Agba signed.

Ethike smiled. *There are no friends beyond the City of Lies,* he replied.

The third story.

For centuries, the Children of Tutu had been subjugated and brutalized and maimed, not just by the Aleke and the ogisi of the City of Lies, but by an unholy alliance of leaders from all over the desert. This third story was the most important. When people of equal power come together, they cooperate. When people of unequal power come together, subjugation begins. Let the people of the Forever Desert fear each other so that they never again form the alliances that lead them to cruelty. Let them never meet the people with the knowledge to unravel the stories they'd been told. Let their own mistrust be the shackles of their prison.

In his years as the city's leader, Agba had wondered many times whether he was doing the right thing. The Ogisi had shown him so much, but he was still just a mortal; there was so much he didn't know. Perhaps if he knew more, he would have found another way. A better way. Perhaps he was making a mistake.

But then he remembered. He remembered Baba's corpse. He remembered all the Children's severed hands hung around their necks. He remembered all that The Ogisi had shown him, how humanity's past was no different from its present.

Lastly, he remembered his time in the desert with Ethike. Remembered how one kind man had shown a young and angry boy that there was power in faith, and that there were times when foolishness— when trusting those who should not be trusted—was perhaps the wisest path.

Agba took a final glance back at the city. It was now dry, empty of trees and water and the beautiful, towering architecture it had once held. Its people were miserable, suffering through the punishment for their centuries of crimes.

But they were alive. Still living and breathing and loving. And as long as they were alive, there was hope. Agba had done what was required to protect the Children of Tutu and create a broader peace in the Forever Desert. But ultimately, he was placing his faith in Ethike and Uwi, and in the people of the city. Maybe someday they would find a better solution, one that allowed everyone to be free and watered and kind.

If that day ever came, he would not be there to see it.

Agba smacked the camels' flanks, spurring the wagon out through the city's iron gates. Before him, the desert's gold dunes drank steaming sunlight and stretched on and on in an endless march, into an eternity that—with each breath of wind—buried beneath its sands the sharp bones and bloated remains of past travelers, shielding the un-calloused feet of those yet to tread upon it and preserving its promise of adventure, its promise of truth, its story with no ending.

ACKNOWLEDGMENTS

I remember, when finishing an early draft of *The Lies of the Ajungo*, feeling like a hypocrite. One of the messages of the book was that those we are led to believe are our enemies are often just people like us. But I conclude the book with the Ajungo as clear, irredeemable villains. They are cruel for no reason, inhuman. It was then that I realized there was more story to tell. Who were the Ajungo? How did they come to be? Where did their three lies come from?

One of the few good things about history repeating itself is that it means there are no true endings or beginnings. Agba's story might come a thousand years after Tutu's story, five hundred years after Osi's. Or it may come thousands of years earlier, after a different Tutu and a different Osi. It could take place in a world shaped by the Ajungo and the Aleke that we know or it could be the origin of those words. It's a sequel—the conclusion—as much as it is a prequel—the inciting incident.

I started this series as a way of navigating the tension between the culture of my ancestry and the culture of my upbringing; Ethike and Agba (and, ultimately, Uwi) are the culmination of that journey. Like them, I don't know if the decisions I made in this book are the best ones, but they're the decisions I can live with, and I'm grateful that I was able to tell this story in full. Still can't believe it, to be honest. But I'm endlessly grateful.

In that vein, I must give thanks to my agent, Jim McCarthy, and my editors, Carl Engle-Laird and Matt Rusin. Writing this series has been one of the most challenging things I've ever done, and these three fabulous souls held my hand through it in such a kind way. I never imagined having so much creative freedom and encouragement in a debut book, but that is what I got when writing the Forever Desert. Truly an honor to work with them, and with the whole publishing team at Tordotcom: my publishers, Irene Gallo, Will Hinton, and Claire Eddy; production editor Dakota Griffin; production manager

Jackie Huber-Rodriguez; the marketing team of Julia Bergen, Michael Dudding, and Sam Friedlander; eagle-eyed copy editor Michelle Li; proofreader NaNá V. Stoelzle; cold reader Madeline Grigg; and publicist and all-around lovely, generous human being Alexis Saarela.

Thank you to my writing group—Woody, Ananda, Alyssa, Rayn, Andre. And to my lifelong writing besties, Cade Hagen and Sarah al-Tamimi, the former of whom has always helped me think through my stories better and the latter of whom has always helped me feel my stories better.

To Alyssa Winans and Christine Foltzer—y'all should be tried for witchcraft for what you did with these covers. I cannot express enough how blown away I am by your artistry. Each cover was better than the last and together they tell the story of the Forever Desert better than I ever could.

Lastly, thanks to you all, the readers. This concludes (or begins) our journey together through the Forever Desert. When I started this, I never really understood that other people would be reading it and connecting with it, but every one of you who has said kind words at an event, tagged me in a social media post, DM'd or emailed me, wrote a review, left a comment on Goodreads (I confess that I have read ALL of them), or just told a friend about these books—you have made my dreams come true. I hope you find this book satisfying in some way, even if you don't agree with all of the decisions I made, and I hope you're able to return again and again to this world anytime you need whatever it is that it has given you.

May we all always find water and shade and be remembered truly.

ABOUT THE AUTHOR

Shoott Photography

MOSES OSE UTOMI is a Nigerian American fantasy writer and nomad currently based out of San Diego, California. He has an MFA in fiction from Sarah Lawrence College and is a winner of the Ignyte Award and the Hurston/Wright Foundation Legacy Award. His work includes the Forever Desert novella trilogy and the Sisters of the Mud young adult duology. When he's not writing, he's traveling, training martial arts, or doing karaoke—with or without a backing track.